Instinctively, I reached to embrace her. My hands fell to my own body but the weight of her remained, shifting against my length like an invisible tide. I raised one knee to ease it. She stopped — confused perhaps? But then she began again, rocking on top of me and against my thigh as the stroking continued, harder, more demanding.

An intensity of energy flashed through the room. The flames flared and danced and in the newfound brightness I saw on the wall the shadow of my body lying prone, and with my shadow rocked another, slender, intent, with a wild unbound cascade of shadow hair. She raised up then and I saw the silhouette of her body, of her breasts. I watched the shadow of my hand reach up to cup her breast and where the shadows met, my hand met nothing. I heard a laugh, not mine, as she turned also to the wall, watching me grasp thin air instead of her. She reached out a hand and I did too. There was nothing tangible, but our shadow hands overlapped against the wall, a cool warmth against my palm. The weight on me shuddered as I had earlier, then fell against me. I felt the tickle of her hair against my nose and a pressure on my lips. There was a breathlike movement at my ear, but it was in my heart I heard the word.

"Forever," she said. "Forever."

About the Author

Molleen Zanger lives in the thumb of Michigan with her mate, her son, three dogs, two cats and a collection of cacti and succulents. She was born in Panama C.Z. and raised in Michigan. Among other things, she has worked as a postal carrier, bartender, real estate sales associate and staff writer-photographer on a weekly newspaper. Other Naiad publications include her first novel, *The Year Seven,* and short stories in: *The Erotic Naiad* and *The Romantic Naiad.*

GARDENIAS WHERE THERE ARE NONE

BY
MOLLEEN ZANGER

The Naiad Press, Inc.
1994

Printed in the United States of America on acid-free paper
First Edition

Edited by Christine Cassidy
Cover design by Pat Tong and Bonnie Liss
    (Phoenix Graphics)
Typeset by Sandi Stancil

Library of Congress Cataloging-in-Publication Data

Zanger, Molleen, 1948–
    Gardenias where there are none / by Molleen Zanger.
        p.   cm.
    ISBN 1-56280-056-6
    1. Lesbians—Midwest (U.S.)—Fiction.   I. Title.
PS3576.A53G37   1994
813'.54—dc20   93-41790
                                                          CIP

*This book is dedicated to my dear MJ
who has learned to just slide the tray
under the door and jump back.*

Acknowledgments

Thanks, as always, to my family — MJ Ogden and Kevin for immediate support, and Stacy and Scott for long-distance support; to my friends for encouragement; and especially to my dear friend Dr. Judy Mimken of Saginaw Valley State University for reading, commenting, critiquing and questioning.

Special thanks, in all sincerity, to all of those who, throughout my life, have done everything in their power to keep me down, to keep me silent, to keep me straight and narrow. Without your influences to resist I might never have known the joy of owning a life worth celebrating.

Chapter 1

"What a dump."

Ford was right, of course, but her remark hurt anyway.

"Yeah, but it has potential," I offered hopefully.

"Oh, sure it does. It has the potential to fall down around your head."

"No, really, come with me," I said, tugging her sleeve and leading her to the basement door.

She hesitated. "Mel, I don't think I want to..."

"It's okay. I want to show you something." I

flipped on the light and led her down the narrow steps.

Ordinarily I don't think about my friend's bulk, but the closeness of the narrow stairway reminded me that Hermana Elizabetta Ford is one large woman. I'd also forgotten her claustrophobia.

"There's a door to the outside down here," I reassured her. "We can go out through there. Careful. The last few steps are loose."

"Wonderful. Just wonderful," Ford muttered, more to herself than to me.

"Now. Look," I said, proudly waving my arms toward the basement ceiling. "Have you ever seen anything like that?"

Ford waited a beat or so.

"What?" she said sarcastically. "The cobwebs? They're nice, Mel, very nice indeed."

I elbowed her. "No, not the cobwebs. The beams."

"They're logs."

"Yes, yes, yes. Logs." I was pleased she finally got it. "They're logs with the bark still on. Aren't they beautiful? See? See how neat it is? These logs were cut and laid in place just the way they fell, without being stripped or shaped or treated. Maybe they were cut right here on the property. Maybe . . ."

But my tremendous discovery hadn't held her attention. She slowly stalked the perimeter of the basement, pausing here and there and shaking her head.

"Ford, don't you get it? Can't you see?" I pleaded.

"Well, babe," she pronounced in that know-it-all voice she gets sometimes, the only times she exasperates me, "what I can see is that the foundation's already been repaired once and not very

2

well. And the wiring is criminal. You can pretty much count on getting fricasseed in your sleep some night. That is, if the foundation doesn't cave in first."

I was really pissed. "The plumbing's all been redone, though," I snapped at her, "and there's a washer and dryer."

Ford lifted the washing machine's lid and peered in cautiously. "Probably broken."

"Well, if it's broken I'll just have to fix it, won't I?"

"Or pay out a fortune to have it done."

I slammed open the outside door I'd promised her and stepped out into waist-high weeds. She followed me up the hill behind the house. We stood for a minute in the sun, my arms crossed defensively across my chest, her hands on her hips. She was examining the roof.

"Tin," she said, "That'll be fun in the rain." But her tone was facetious and I didn't respond. Finally she said, "Well, I sure wouldn't buy this place — at any price."

Trying to control my anger, I stiffly answered, "I'm not buying it, Ford, I'm renting it. And I like it. A lot. I love it, in fact. I think it's perfect. And I'm going to fix it up."

"With what? A pint of gas and a match?"

Speechless at her lack of vision and sensitivity, I just glared at her.

"Mel, just promise me one thing, will you? Promise me you won't sink any lower than this, no matter what."

I glared some more, but she ignored me and kept on talking, making it worse.

3

"You know, I don't even understand why you want to live this far out from town. Getting to school in the winter will be a bitch."

"It's only a forty-five-minute drive."

"It's a forty-five-minute drive for me. The way you drive, it'll take an hour. That's two hours, every day. For what?"

"I like it out here. I like this house."

"Well, you're welcome to it. And if it doesn't work out . . . well, you can always move back in with me, you know. I loved having you around, Mel."

I took her last remark as a sort of apology, or at least an explanation, for her lack of support.

"Look," I said, "it was always the plan for me to get my own place. I need my own space, quiet, you know."

"Well, this much quiet would drive me nuts."

"Any quiet would drive you nuts," I teased, trying to lighten the tension between us. Ford was my best friend and I didn't want to mar that connection.

After a moment, she said, "Well, if it's quiet you want, I guess you've got it. Hell, you could hear a bird fart out here. I just wish it wasn't such a dump."

With a sigh, I offered the one explanation she could possibly accept. "The rent is right."

"I would certainly hope so. But look, I gotta get. Gimme one." She opened her arms wide for a hug, then ambled off to her truck and, waving continuously, drove off.

What I'd said about the rent was true. I was paying considerably less than I'd budgeted for this year. But that was the least of the factors in my decision to move here. Actually, I knew I wanted to live here from the moment I laid my hand against the gray clapboard siding and promised to return.

Or was it from the first glimpse of the inside as I peered, my hands shielding the glare of the sun, into the front bedroom window?

Or was it from the moment I saw it, perched on the hill, overlooking the highway, the branches of its willow tree waving to me in the wind, catching my attention?

Maybe the house was calling me even before that. Certainly I wasn't looking for a place to stay that far out of Adrian. I had planned to rent a room or apartment within walking distance to my graduate classes at the college. I imagined long hours at the research library, long days in front of my word processor, and Saturday nights at the new girl-bar in the heart of town.

Except for those wind-whipped willow branches, I probably would not have even noticed my house, my home. I can't explain what I was doing that far into the country. Ford was fine with me sleeping on her couch until I found my own place. Our tolerance for mess was similar even if our tolerance for noise wasn't.

Ford lives continually surrounded with sound. She sleeps with her television on, listens to the radio, tapes or compact discs during all waking hours. Her phone is seldom silent and when she isn't listening to something or someone, she is talking. She will talk to anyone at anytime about anything. It is truly amazing, and truly exhausting to me.

So there I was, trapped at Ford's, a week from starting classes, and frustrated at not being able to find a place that didn't smell of cat piss or a decade's worth of cigarette smoke. Having cleaned Ford's refrigerator twice in one week, I decided to burn off my energy by exploring the area.

I headed north. Subie, my old gray Subaru wagon with her duct-taped left front fender, had a full tank of gas and I had a $20 bill. Anything was possible.

I felt lucky. And I was. Not only had I been accepted in the newly established graduate program in creative writing at Adrian College and would be near my best buddy, Ford, but I'd won a fellowship which paid me enough to live on for a year and waived my tuition and all fees. Plus, all this happened just when my dad took an early out from Steering Gear in Saginaw and my folks decided to sell everything and move to Florida. Which left me without a place to go for Sunday dinner or the occasional emergency cupboard raid.

They'd told me they were waiting until I graduated from college, but I hadn't realized they meant almost to the day. They'd paid my tuition for five years at Saginaw Valley State University, but I paid my own rent and expenses by working at one video store or another. I loved telling people I worked in film: "...I rent it." The exposure to different kinds of people also helped my writing. I kept an ongoing journal with character sketches, hoping I could use them some day.

I'd had a few short stories published by the campus literary magazine, and one poem, but when it came time to submit samples with my grad school application, I'd sent in an odd little piece about falling asleep. I anguished over the decision. Should I have chosen one of the published ones? I knew I'd made a mistake in only applying to Adrian; I knew I should have asked for a recommendation letter from a professor who'd gone to Adrian, but he was such a prick, I just couldn't do it.

Then the letters came. Accepted by Adrian. Granted a fellowship. What more could I ask? I was the luckiest dyke in Michigan. All I had to do now was work my ass off writing. But first I had to find a quiet place to live that would not kick up my allergies. Sharing Ford's apartment was just not possible.

Two miles from the US-127 — US-12 junction, the road curved and declined sharply. Harald Highway, really just a short dirt road, joined US-12 right at that curve. With so much potential for limited visibility, I would never have looked up the embankment to the left if it hadn't been for the willow whips tossed by the wind.

Sometimes I fall in love with trees. Not collectively, individually. I loved the Russian Olive tree my folks planted in their front yard the week I was born. I loved a catalpa tree in someone's front yard that I passed every day on my way to school, even taking a series of pictures of it through the seasons. I marked a spot on the sidewalk with spray paint so I'd get the exact same angle for each shot. I never took a picture of my grandmother's oak tree, which I now regret. Its breastlike burls comforted me many times as I suffered some childish anguish or other. There was a ginkgo tree in downtown Jackson, just outside the only gay bar, and a weeping mulberry that I met outside of the China exhibition at Epcot Center during a Florida vacation.

The wind blew the untrimmed willow wands

toward the road and away from the windows of the small house. An orange sign in the left front window read "For Rent." There was a line of black printing I surmised was a phone number, but I couldn't read it from the road.

I hadn't thought much before about making a home of my own. Subie seemed like my home — we'd been together for over five years — bought used with my high school graduation take. She was with me through my college years and my Rebecca era which coincided with my senior year. For Subie's loyalty she'd received a new transmission, two sets of new tires and innumerable oil changes which I did myself every three thousand miles, no matter what. We were comfortable together and she was paid for. I felt at ease behind her wheel and I knew just what I could and could not expect from her. She had been all the home I needed until I met the house. And Camille, who came later, or rather, came to me later, for she had been there long before me.

When I saw the orange sign and felt that leap of expectation in my solar plexus, I executed an awkward and illegal U-turn to find the driveway up to the house. I needed that phone number. It took two more U-turns before I figured out that the driveway was shared for the first five feet with a green cinder-block house 150 feet or so west of the little gray one. Then the driveway split into two with the one I wanted running parallel to the highway and skirting the rise of the embankment. The grass was long and there was no sidewalk except for the last few feet before the porch steps which led to the side door — clearly used as the main entrance.

The house was nothing to look at: small, gray with white trim and a dull tin roof. The landscaping was minimal — a couple of mock-orange bushes flanked the seldom-used front door. Its only memorable trait was its nearness to the road. It was exactly thirty feet from the highway: fifteen feet up and fifteen feet back.

Peering into one of the front windows, I saw a small room wallpapered in green on white print, something geometric. The other front window showed me two empty rooms divided by a wide archway. The other windows were too high to peer into since the land fell sharply away toward the back of the house and continued its downward slope past a small gray barn, trimmed, like the house, in white. The nearest house to the east was at the bottom of the hill and far enough away that the pickup truck in its driveway looked like a Matchbox replica.

The back and side yards gave way to the neighbor's fenced-in horse pasture where several reddish brown horses stood stoically facing into the wind. I'm not a horse person, but their manes and tails flickering in the wind made me smile.

To the south, across the highway, was a small cement plant owned, I would later learn, by people who lived nestled next to the plant itself. But from where I stood all I could see were a tall tower and gray mounds.

To the north were uninhabited woods, then wetlands. Beyond them lay Goose Creek on the farther shore of which stood the old abandoned cement plant that gave Cement City, the nearest village, its name. In the winter, when the leaves were off the trees, I would be able to see the towers of the old plant in the distance, but on this first day I saw only trees and the barn. The nearest neighbors, in the green cinder block house to the west, were far enough away to preserve the feeling of privacy.

It was so quiet. The quiet entered and calmed me. It should not have seemed quiet with the highway so close. Maybe the embankment muffled the road noise, or maybe I was already falling in love with the house and was ready to disregard any shortcomings. Whatever the reason, I felt at peace there, and at home.

With a pen and an old envelope I scrounged from Subie's glove compartment, I walked through the tall grass and wrote down the number on the sign. But before I left to find a pay phone, I placed my open right palm against the old gray house and promised to return.

Chapter 2

"How much for the house?" I asked the woman who answered. My rising excitement blew all social norms right out of my mind.

"I can show it to you in an hour," was her unsatisfactory reply.

I didn't need to see it; I needed to know how much the rent was. My budget was tight, but I was ready to go higher if I had to. I wanted that house and was even prepared to give up a luxury or two — my book club membership, for example, or three meals a day. Two would suffice. Let's see, I calculated, a carton of yogurt a day was ... not enough. Pepsi. Could I give up my one addiction? Cut back, maybe? Maybe have one on Sundays? How much would that save?

"Hello?" the woman prompted, bringing me back to the corner bar I'd called from. "Would that be all right? I'll meet you there with the key in an hour."

She didn't wait for confirmation but hung up. Talking to the disconnected phone, I said, "But you didn't tell me how much."

Then I replaced the receiver and threw a wave and a smile at the cute bartender. "Thanks," I said for no particular reason. I had, after all, paid for the call.

That bartender was pretty dykey. It would be nice to meet the neighborhood sisters, but the cigarette smoke was strong and I was too antsy to sit still for an hour. So I left to return to my house.

In my imagination, it was my house already, which is why I didn't hesitate to explore. The barn was particularly alluring and the wall-sized door slid begrudgingly in its track.

My eyes quickly adjusted to the dark interior and the first thing I saw was a couple of old dressers. Their drawers were full of empty canning jars, quarts and pints, but that was all. What was I hoping for? Secrets? Clues to previous residents? Well, now I knew one thing for sure — someone who lived here at some time or other did canning, or had intended to. I laughed at my own mock mystery. There was nothing mysterious about canning jars and dressers. Nor was there anything mysterious about the stack of gray barnwood against one wall, a few bald tires and an old crescent wrench rusted to a solid piece. There was a loft over half the barn. A ladder with a third of its rungs missing led up to it, but judging from what I could see by standing on tiptoe and craning my neck, there was nothing up there but discarded boards and old, half-rotted window frames. None of which was interesting enough to risk broken bones on that dilapidated ladder.

Through a broken floorboard, I caught a glimpse of a room below. Like the house, the barn was set into a hill and the lower level, I found, was as cool as it was dark. I saw no light switch or pullcord, so I didn't go too deeply into the room. There seemed to be more broken and abandoned house and car parts, and also some pieces of rusted machinery which had obviously not performed their intended functions in a very long time — whatever those intended functions might be.

As I turned to leave, I spotted a slab of wood propped by the doorway. It was a large piece of driftwood, flat on one side but rounded on the other with several knots. I touched that smooth wood appreciatively; like living trees, driftwood fascinated me. It was the only thing I saw in the lower level of any interest or value.

Stepping back out into the sun, I noticed a pair of T-shaped clothesline posts behind the barn and, halfway up the hill to the house, a large cylindrical object — an old water heater, I guessed. Apparently they'd installed a new one recently, and hadn't removed the old one.

I climbed up to it and was wondering what it would take to either get it hauled away or roll it down the hill and out of sight behind the barn when

I heard a car pull up. Eagerly, I went to meet my new landlady.

From the start I assumed the house was mine, that I was supposed to live here, and I approached the woman with just that attitude.

Sticking out my hand, I said, "Hi, I'm Melanie Myer. Thanks for meeting me on such short notice."

"I'm Louise Madison," she said, dropping my hand quickly and striding toward the house, keys in hand.

Besides what Ford calls our "gaydar," the thing that made me think this woman was a lesbian was how ridiculous she looked in the outfit she wore. A hideous green and brown paisley polyester housedress that even my grandmother would have refused to wear, it fit her as if she were a linebacker. Her hair was short, cut in a no-nonsense anti-style, and she wore no makeup except for a thickly applied, garish coral lipstick. Wearing sensible stacked-heel walking shoes, she strode to the house as if she were more accustomed to hiking boots.

After the initial handshake, she refused to meet my gaze and was careful to keep a good arm's-length distance from me. Closet case, I figured, having dealt with them before. Probably not even out to herself, I thought, as she unlocked the side door.

"You can look around if you want. I'll wait here," she said. It wasn't until much later that I realized she seemed more nervous than most "innies" stuck alone with an "outie" (Ford's terms). But I didn't pay that much attention at the time; I was too absorbed in the discovery of my house. She waited by the side door. The kitchen was long and narrow, with a brown refrigerator and a green electric stove that were clean but beat-up. A door led from the kitchen to the dining room — the room in which I'd already decided to set up my word processor. At the near end of the dining room was a narrow closet and a tiny bathroom with a fairly new shower and tub enclosure, toilet and diminutive sink on thin rickety chrome legs. Above the sink was a standard medicine cabinet with a mirrored door. Everything was clean but dusty and ordinary . . . except for the horrendous flowered contact paper someone had used for wallpaper.

Toward the front of the house was the living room, bare even of curtains. Through another doorway was the bedroom I'd peered into earlier. Now the wallpaper appeared white with green and I realized the optical illusion. Depending on the angle from which it was seen, the paper looked either green on white or white on green. I took the "For Rent" sign out of the window and carried it with me up the short, narrow staircase to the upper level. There were two tiny rooms up there, the back one approachable only through the front one. Because of the slope of the roof, there wasn't much room to stand. Where the ceilings sloped sharply, I had to bend over.

It was more house than I needed but I was smiling the whole time. So what if the wallpaper in the stairwell was buckled and peeled, or the plaster gaped in the ceiling in the bedroom and on the walls in the living room? Yes, the wood floors were dull and stained. Yes, the windows were long unwashed and possibly unwashable because they were painted shut. I also saw the hand-hewn beams along the length of the living room ceiling — adz marks clear and irregularly spaced. I could imagine the solid thunk of the tool against the logs, squaring them into beams. I could imagine the vibration in the air from each blow. I felt warm and safe and ... wanted. This house wanted me here. This was where I belonged.

Returning to the kitchen, I handed Louise Madison the sign. "I'll take it," I said, then noticed another door off the kitchen. "Where does that door go?"

"The basement," she said, still avoiding my eyes.

"Can I see that, too?"

"No. I mean, there's nothing to see. It's just a basement." She moved out onto the porch where she seemed to straighten. And strengthen. "Well, when do you want to move in?" She fiddled with the keys in her hand.

"Immediately. Today. I'd like to get settled in before school starts next week ..."

"You teach?" she asked with the first sign of interest and the first voluntary eye contact.

I hated to disappoint her.

"No. I'm a student. At Adrian. Grad school. A new program in ..."

"Oh," she said, disinterested immediately. "I always wanted to be a teacher."

"Why didn't you?"

"Will you be living here alone?" she asked, ignoring my question.

I can play that game. "Can you tell me anything about the house?"

She looked startled. "Like what?"

"Like, how old it is, its history."

"Well, not really. Not much. It's my mother's house really. I just . . . take care of things for her. She's not well and . . . she's old. She knows all about it but . . . I do know the back half, from the dining room back, is new. Like the forties I think. The old part was originally a log cabin, for hired help to live in when this land was one big farm. Our house — Mother's house — is the original farmhouse. We live just two doors down, a quarter of a mile. The green house next door was built in the fifties by my uncle — my father's brother — deeded to him as a gift, then he sold it to the Greens who still live there . . ."

"My neighbors in the green house are named Green? I love it."

"They're retired now, nice people, go to Texas every winter to stay with a daughter and her family. Anyway," she said with a little shake of her head and a small smile, "you'll need these."

She handed me the keys, careful not to actually touch me. The metal was warm from her hand.

"Aren't you forgetting something?" I asked.

She looked at me quizzically.

"Money?" I offered.

"Oh, yes, of course. Let's see, we'll have to get more for it this time. We have to pay for the new plumbing, the new septic system. Mother's medication. How about two seventy-five?"

"You mean two hundred and seventy-five dollars? A month?" I'd expected four, four-fifty, maybe more.

"Well, okay, make it two-fifty." She turned to walk away.

"Wait. I . . . I don't have the money on me, I have to go . . ."

"The yellow house. On the other side of the green one, just down a piece. You can drop it off. I have to get home now. I can't leave Mother alone."

Briskly she strode to her car, a lumbering older-model Pontiac in pristine condition. I had to run to catch up to her.

"Mrs. Madison, wait. Did you ... have you ever lived in this house?"

What made me ask that question? It had no bearing on anything. I felt foolish as she looked at me, through me, it seemed.

Finally she answered, nodding as she spoke. "Yes. Yes, I did. For a while. Years ago. But ... I wasn't comfortable. Women ... women are not usually comfortable here. I'd feel better if you were a man," she said, turning abruptly. She got in her car and eased away, barely disturbing the dust in the driveway.

Ignoring her apparent sexism, I turned back to the house. Fondling the keys and smiling, I said aloud, "Hi honey, I'm home."

Chapter 3

In high spirits, I drove back to Ford's for my checkbook and whatever Subie would hold, especially my futon mattress. Bought at a yard sale for $10 without a frame, it is nowhere near comfy, but better than a sleeping bag for emergency sleepovers. This was, I decided, definitely an emergency: I had to sleep in my house that night.

Ford was still at work, managing the golf course her parents own, and my original note was still on her kitchen table. I added a p.s. with the latest development, an invitation, directions and a request to bring out a load of my stuff if she came.

Then I jammed the essentials into Subie: my clothes, word processor; a cardboard file box of office supplies, and the wooden folding TV tray set that I used as a four-section desk, the matching chair that kills my butt when I type for long periods. There were two boxes — one marked *kitchen* — big and bulky — and another smaller one marked *bathroom.* Garbage bags held towels, sheets and my afghans — nearly two dozen of them.

Every year of my life my grandmother has given me an afghan for Christmas, and I still have them all except the orange and brown ripple one a former roommate stole and the black lacy one Ford fell in love with. I gave her that one for her last birthday. The whole collection fits into four lawn and leaf bags. I grabbed one of the bags at random, hoping for the one with the pink flowers. I thought the house would like it.

Home. What a word for me to fall in love with. *Home.* I was alive with the possibility of being at home, coming home, going home, making a home, homemaking, homecoming, home-going, home-having. As I drove I made a mental list of things I wanted to do to the house.

Pulling into the landlady's driveway, I wondered briefly whether I should go to the front or side door, but she solved my dilemma by opening the side one and leaning out. Checkbook in hand, I approached her.

"Look, I'm on a fellowship and the money is disbursed in chunks, so would it be all right if I paid for six months in advance? I could pay for a year but . . ."

She looked at the check I'd made out. "Of course," she said. She seemed dazed. "That will be fine."

It would be even more fine, I figured, once the check cleared.

Unsmiling, she began to retreat into the house.

"I have a couple of questions, though," I said.

She looked at me warily.

"I noticed an old dresser in the barn. Could I use it? I don't have much furniture and . . ."

Visibly relieved, she nodded. "Yes, yes, of course. Use anything you find. There's a washer and dryer in the basement, too. You're welcome to use it. Anything you find."

"And barnwood. There's some barnwood out back. Could I use it to build a bookshelf?"

"Yes, yes, of course."

"And there are some other things." I wanted to patch some plaster, refinish the wood floors in the living and dining rooms, and paint the bathroom. I was careful not to disparage the wallpaper in case she'd chosen it herself.

She looked at me oddly for a minute, then shook her head. I thought I'd overstepped my role as tenant and she was going to tell me no, but instead she said, "There's no problem with any of that but . . . about your check . . . if you decide not to stay, well, I'll . . . we'll refund the remainder."

"I intend to stay. I love the house."

"But you haven't —" She stopped herself. "Well, don't hesitate to ask. You do whatever you want, I mean, you aren't going to paint the rooms black or anything are you?"

I laughed and assured her I preferred light, neutral colors. Then a bell rang from inside the house.

"Mother," she explained. "I have to go." The screen door closed and she retreated into the dimness of the house.

"Wait, please, do you think I could talk to her sometime, about the house, I mean. You said she —"

"No. No, I'm sorry. I don't see how that's possible. She . . . well, she isn't . . . She doesn't think right anymore. Maybe if she . . . but I doubt it. She's very old, very confused. It's . . . difficult."

"Well, are there any pictures of the house? Before, I mean? Before it was sided? When it was log? I'd really love to see —"

The bell rang again, longer and more insistently. Her face showed a deepening distress.

Hurriedly she said, "I don't think so. I've never seen any. I don't know. I'll look around. I have to go now."

She moved out of sight and I turned away from the empty doorway.

Then I went home to unload, to empty the dresser's drawers and wrestle it up the hill from the barn to the porch where I washed it down. I wiped out the kitchen cupboards and put away my few things. I set up my word processor — "Rosa", I call her — which is really just a glorified typewriter. Exhausted, I lay down on the futon, but was only there a few minutes when I was up again, ripping that horrid paper off the bathroom walls.

And I smiled. I smiled the whole time. And I

talked to the house which I thought of as female. First I commiserated with her for being ignored, slighted and badly decorated. I told her my plans for replastering, painting, refinishing the floors. I discussed curtains, bookshelves, what I was going to do about furniture. I explained the joys of rummage sales.

Long after midnight I fell fully clothed onto my mattress. Did I eat? Did I drink? I didn't know, could not remember.

A welcome breeze through the house thankfully cooled me. I felt feverish, and thought I might be coming down with something. I smelled a vaguely familiar flower-sweet perfume and I fell asleep trying to identify it. *Not roses, not violets, not lavender, not carnations, not lilies-of-the-valley, not . . .*

Chapter 4

"Eat first, work later," Ford said.

She'd brought out the rest of my stuff and a mushroom pizza that was cold by the time she got there — just the way we like it. She even remembered my side order of anchovies, although I had to endure her usual disparaging of comments.

"Eeuwwww," she began, as always. "You and your dead fish."

"Dead fish *and* fungus," I corrected her, popping an atomic-bomb-cloud-shaped morsel in my mouth.

"Well," she said, her face smoothing into humor

as I continued, undeterred in my methodical arranging of anchovies on each of my slices. "You know what they say: a woman who'll eat anchovies will eat anything."

"Guilty as charged," I leered happily at her, hoping there was food between my teeth.

Our routine seldom varied. It was a way to establish that all was well between us despite whatever else might be going to hell in our lives or the world.

We were sitting with our backs against adjoining walls in my living room. Our legs were stretched out, feet almost meeting, the pizza box within reach.

"So," she said, "have you heard from Bek?"

"No," I answered, "and I don't expect to. Or want to for that matter."

I'd met Bek at the beginning of my senior year of college when, on a whim, I'd strolled a pricey car lot, pretending what I'd do if I won the lottery. She was working there and gave me her business card, saying "Call me — anytime — I mean it!" I'd flirted with her, outrageously, and later couldn't get her off my mind. Her commanding tone as she ordered me to call excited me. Fool that I was, I mistook arrogance for self-assurance. Within the time we were together, I came to know the difference. I also came to hate the smell, the taste and even the sight of alcohol. She always came to my apartment armed with a twelve-pack and at first I thought it was me, that there was something about me that made her need to drink so much. Until I saw how she lived. Then I made excuses for her, tolerated and forgave everything, took it all until I was hollowed out. One spring day she showed up at my door and it was as if I didn't know her, didn't recognize her at all. And didn't care to.

"You're really over her?" asked Ford.

"Yeah, well, I was over her long before we broke up. I know that now. I just needed a while to detox. You know, get her out of my system."

"So you're really over her?"

"Yes, Ford, I am really over her."

"Can I finally tell you what I really thought of your being with her?"

"You mean," I said, trying to look incredulous, "you didn't like her?"

"Do people like mad dogs?"

"That's a little harsh."

"Well, maybe. I just couldn't see what you saw in her, you know, what you were getting out of it. She was so . . . beneath you."

"I never felt —"

"I know, I know. You wouldn't. But I did. I wanted better for you than some proverbial drunken lout."

"Look, Ford —"

"No. Let me finish. After a while I saw that you weren't looking to get anything out of it. I started to think that maybe it wasn't about you, about what might or might not be good for you. It was about her, about your being good *for* her, showing her how to be a person, sort of — teaching her some social skills."

"You mean like which fork to use?"

"No, more like how to use a fork at all."

We laughed and I tossed a wadded-up napkin at her.

"It wasn't that bad, Ford, and it wasn't her fault.

Her parents crippled her, maybe deliberately. They practically infantilized her so they could keep their 'baby.' They're all weird."

"You told me they had a strange house."

"Yeah. They kept buying all this stuff. If it was a good price, they'd buy it, even though they didn't need it or want it, whatever it was. Tools or small appliances for the kitchen, electronic stuff or outdoor equipment for camping or yard work — only they never used any of it. They'd store it, still in cartons, all over their house. It was like a warehouse in there. Boxes and boxes of stuff stacked to the ceiling, in room after room. They were like a family of those spiders that encase their prey and stack them for future use, and there's Bek — an only child — just like one of those bound and gagged, anesthetized, stored-up victims. I almost felt like that was what she wanted to do to me, too. Keep me in this narrow cubicle in case she needed me someday. Only I couldn't figure out what it was she thought she might need me for."

"Sex?"

"Well, yes, sure, there was that but..." I hesitated, it was one thing to laugh and joke about my sex life or lack of it, but serious discussions made me uncomfortable.

Ford was still waiting expectantly, nibbling remnants of bottom crust from the last edge. She never eats the edge crust.

"It's like that," I said, pointing to her mound of edges. "The sexual part of me was the only part she wanted. But the crust — the part that is the real me, that gives me shape and form — well, that didn't interest her. That was dispensable, disposable. For

27

all the time we spent together, we never really talked, never had a real conversation. Not once."

Ford looked at me in disbelief.

"I got hungry, eventually, for conversation. We almost broke up. Oh, hell, we spent our whole time together almost breaking up. But this one time, near the end, I told her we needed to talk more if we were going to make it work. Ha. Make what work? Anyway, we went out to dinner; she took me out to dinner. Feed me or fuck me, that was about it. Anyway, she took me to a restaurant that she'd been to with her parents the night before — they never ate at home, ever. Every single night they ate out. Anyway, we were at this same restaurant, the same table even, she told me. And she started telling me what each of them had ordered — what Ma'd had, what Pa'd had, what she'd had; how it was cooked and how it was served and in what amount of time. Then she told me how each of them had evaluated their meal, if it was cooked right, tasted right, met their expectations. She told me what the bill came to and how much they tipped the waitress. And I just sat there staring at her, listening to her tell me all these things. Then when she was done I said 'Becca, why are you telling me all this?' And she said, 'Well, you said we needed to talk more.'"

I thought about that night. It was one of the last times I saw her. That dinner highlighted our differences like nothing else had. To let her believe I'd started sleeping with someone else was the one thing I knew would drive her away for good.

"One night I woke up to find her standing over

my bed with her fists raised. She wanted to beat me up. She just shoved me around but she wanted to use her fists on me."

"You should have called the cops, Mel."

"Maybe, but I just couldn't. She was pitiful, pathetic. Her rage seemed so puny compared to the strength I felt in being able to go forward with the break-up. I felt powerful. Somehow I resisted the urge to pull her down onto the bed with me. And I wanted to. Even then. With not one other thing in common, with knowing full well what a disaster we were together, I still felt attracted to her. I was so glad to move away from Saginaw before she showed up again."

When I moved in with Ford, it had been three months since I'd seen Becca. I half expected her to show up again, on my doorstep again, crying and wanting me. Yet there were times I knew I wouldn't have been able to say no.

After awhile, Ford gathered up our crumpled napkins, threw everything in the pizza box and took it to the kitchen.

"Well, girl," she said as she returned, "you know what's missing from this party?"

"Wine, women and song?"

"Nope. Tears. That is the first time you have talked about that woman without crying. Congratulations. You made it. You are now officially Done With the Bitch. Come and get your hug."

Which I did.

* * * * *

We unloaded her truck after the pizza had settled.

"Hey, you've still got it," I said, tracing the white vinyl tape cross that joins the bottom of the *O* of *Ford* on her Ranger's tailgate.

"Yup. I figure half the people in Adrian don't know what a woman's symbol is and half of the other half don't know what it means. Half of the half that do know what it means don't know what it means when an uppity woman is sporting one, but half of the half that do know needs to know how to find me."

She swears the tailgate with her name emblazoned on it was not a factor in the decision to buy her truck, but it didn't take us long to personalize it even further.

"What the hell is in these boxes, anyway?" she asked. "Oh, never mind, I know. Books, right?"

"Yes, Ford, books. What else? Furniture I leave behind, women I leave behind, but books are with me always. Someday I'm going to design a bed of books, a table of books, chairs of books . . ."

"That reminds me. I didn't have room for it this trip but my landlady got a new couch and put hers out for the trash. I asked her for it for you and pulled it back into the garage. There's nothing wrong with it but ugly. It's like a sofabed but it doesn't open up. The back flattens out instead. It's pretty cool."

"But ugly?"

"You fussy?"

"I can put a sheet over it."

"Good idea. Sheesh, I can't believe this. First a whole house, now fussy about furniture. What's happening to you? But look, my landlady said to let her know if there's anything else you need. She's got a lot of stuff stored in the garage and the basement that she said you could use. You know, I really believe she's got a crush on you."

"Mrs. Belmont? I only met her once or twice, Ford. Sheesh yourself."

"Once is enough to start a crush. Too bad she's not your type, Mel . . ."

"You mean like lesbian and under seventy?"

"Don't be so narrow-minded. I didn't know you were an ageist."

"Ageist? Hell, I'm just concerned about being able to keep up. You repress a woman that long and then she comes out . . . watch out."

Ford laughed, but I agreed to accept any household goodies my alleged admirer chose to bestow, and Ford offered to bring them out next trip.

When we were done, I pulled us each a quart canning jar of cold tea out of the fridge. I had made "sun tea" without the sun, putting two tea bags in each jar, filling it with cold water and putting it in the refrigerator overnight. *Voila!* Sunless tea, already poured.

Ford got me into tea-drinking; she was seldom without a jug of it nearby, but the individual servings were my latest idea.

"Clever," she said, downing half of hers in one long pull. "And speaking of clever . . . did I tell you about this kid that works for me?"

I groaned, knowing another of her stories was coming. In college she prefaced these stories with "There's this kid in my class who is so dumb . . ." or "There's this guy at work who is so dumb . . ." Now

31

it's a kid who works for her. I never quite believe these stories, but never quite disbelieve them either.

She went on, "This kid is so dumb. He lives with his folks — he's still in high school, a third-year senior — but he's got this dog, a shepherd that he thinks the world of. So he knows he's got to give this dog heartworm medicine — pills, you know. So he leaves the bottle on the kitchen windowsill above the sink so he remembers to give them to his dog every day. But his mom doesn't like the bottle there because it's brown and her kitchen is all blue and white. So she puts the pills in another bottle, a white one, only it's an empty Excedrin bottle. So this kid comes home with a headache and takes two of the heartworm pills, which he does notice are pretty hard to swallow. So when his mom comes in, he complains that she bought the wrong size Excedrin, they were too big."

"Good God, Ford."

"No, wait, I'm not done. So when his mom figures out what he did, she freaks out and calls the vet. The vet asks how much the kid weighs and then tells them not to worry — he took the right dosage for his size."

We both laughed, then lapsed into that companionable silence that is so easy with Ford.

I was about to ask what new woman was on her horizon — there is always at least one in a holding pattern at any given moment — when Ford started sniffing, a quizzical expression on her face.

"Mel," she said, "do you have some kind of air freshener thing going or something?"

I shook my head. I knew what was coming.

"Then what is that smell? Sweet. Perfumey.

Flowers. Some kind of flowers. A woman! Mel, you sneaky devil you. Have you got a woman tucked away here somewhere?"

"Well," I said, getting self-conscious. "Not exactly. Um . . . the house is kind of strange, when I was unpacking, I noticed hot spots, cold spots, and — It's almost as if there are moods in the air. I can feel them. And there's the flower smell. I can't quite figure out what flower that is. I almost think I should know, but —"

Ford cut me off. "Are you telling me you think the house is haunted? Yeah, right." She laughed heartily and I smiled shamefacedly.

She was right. It was foolish. But still, the flowery smell was even stronger and there was that strange feeling, the one I'd felt since I first found the house. Accompanied. That was it. I felt accompanied.

Chapter 5

My dreams changed. Not gradually as I settled into my new surroundings, but abruptly, from the first night.

Ordinarily my dreams, like everyone else's, I suppose, were repositories of images, thoughts or emotions that my mind had collected like a huge nondiscriminating electromagnet. Like a landfill artist making mosaics out of trash or weavings out of waste, my mind sorted through these random images and displayed them nightly. They were fairly simple to identify: an overheard comment, a visual image from a TV show, a passage from a book that took root subliminally.

Only occasionally would a dream elude me. These I ascribed to the universal human fears of loss, rejection, failure, death.

But now my dreams had a common theme. In these dreams I wandered. There was a sense of search, but a half-hearted search, a search that was assuredly useless but which must be performed. In these dreams I wandered through corridors, through rooms opening onto rooms which opened onto other rooms. I wandered through deserted streets, down darkened sidewalks and unending alleyways. I wandered through fields, through woods, across beaches, ever seeking something I knew I would not find. There were no colors in these dreams, no sounds, no other people. There was nothing but the wandering itself, futile and endless. And I did not know, upon waking, what these dreams meant.

Once awake, I was too busy to wonder.

The bookshelves were first. I made them out of barnwood sawn to fit the west wall of the living room and braced on metal brackets — a crude method, but one I liked once finished. The rough, gray, weathered wood was beautiful. I used more of the same wood to make a crude coffee table with two old apple crates I found in the lower level of the barn. The unused apparatus there turned out to be an old apple press, and piled in the farthest, darkest corner were dozens of slatted gray wood crates.

I carried the driftwood up to the house, too,

rigging it with screw eyes and wire like a picture frame and hanging it in the living room.

Around my desk I hung the pictures that meant the most to me — a watercolor collage of a white trillium, done by my friend Kathleen and a tapestry weaving of hers that could be a tornado, lightning, a cardiogram or a line of clouds along the horizon, depending on how I hung it. Nearby I positioned my degree, matted and framed (which is what I liked telling people I intended to do with it, when they asked); my framed cover of the 1993 Lesbian *Newsweek*; and a framed but totally fake letter from Whoopi telling me it was all over between us because I was a bum fuck and could not even cook. This was Ford's idea of a prank birthday gift though she didn't expect me to display it with such pride.

I hung white lace curtains on the bottom half of the dining room windows and bought rice paper blinds for the living room and front bedroom, where I'd moved my futon. I bought bleach, sandpaper and polyurethane by the gallon for the floors. I painted the bathroom and hung a white lace curtain at the bottom half of that window too. I wanted to look out at the fields, the woods, the hills. No one could see in, and after all, there was no one out there to look. I bought huge plastic wood-grained house numbers, painted them bright red and installed them on the outside of the house so they could be seen easily by rescue crews if Ford's predictions of disaster proved true.

There was no end to it. Before one task was half completed, two more would pop into my head.

Other things did, too. If I misplaced a tool or a book, anything, all I had to do was close my eyes and relax and the image would come to me of where exactly it was. If I raced around searching, rooting through drawers or boxes, I could never find it. But as soon as I closed my eyes and relaxed, I would get that image, and know.

Sometimes I said thanks.

Sometimes I felt "You're welcome."

More and more often I felt the warmth, the slight pressures or strokes, like gentle caresses on my face, my arms — once on the back of my shoulder. I still smelled the flowers and I still could not identify them.

Chapter 6

Eagerly, I started school the last week of August. I was registered for a class in feminist philosophy, one in feminist literature, and the all-important writing workshop.

The writing prof was a dyke. I knew that from scuttlebutt, but one look would have told me. She was gorgeous, too. Things were definitely promising on my first day of class. I always do better in classes where I can work up a slight crush on the prof. The first glimpse of her swing of shiny blonde pageboy, worn jeans, chambray shirt and shit-kicking boots assured the requisite crush.

Brashly, stupidly, possibly to impress her with my fearlessness which I did not really feel, I volunteered to be the first to submit a story for workshopping. I knew how this worked — had done it many times, seven, in fact, eight if you counted the poetry one. Each class member was to submit two short stories at two separate times during the term. We would each make as many photocopies of our story as there were class members, plus one for the professor. The stories were critiqued and returned with comments and suggestions for revision which were discussed in class. The only difference here was that the student whose story was being workshopped was to remain silent — was considered "dead."

And I went first.

I chose a brand-new story about flirting at a lesbian Halloween party and brought thirteen copies to the next session. With my stomach feeling like a swarm of bees had taken up residence, I went to the next class.

A young guy spoke first, "Well, I didn't like having to work so hard to figure out who are the women and who are the men . . ."

"Men?" interrupted an older guy with white hair who was barely in control of his rage. "There are no men in this piece. This is just a smutty little story about a lesbian drag party . . ."

A drag party? Halloween as drag? I longed to defend myself, opened my mouth to do so.

"Nuh uh, Melanie," the beautiful Professor Burnside said, "You're dead."

So I sat silent as this old guy raged on. "If you're going to succeed in getting the money out of my pocket for your stories, you're going to have to write something I want to read and I don't want to read this trash. You'd better keep that in mind in the future."

Others spoke, a few weakly defending me but not my story. In bitter, silent humiliation I sat, listening. No one addressed issues of style, of narrative tone, or of character integrity. I knew I had a problem writing each character's dialogue so it was distinct from the others. Why didn't someone talk about that, or continuity. All they wanted to do was be able to tell the girls from the boys.

Then another woman spoke, another dyke, I was sure. "Yeah, that business of them all just waiting for their turn in the bathroom to do each other really offended me. It reinforces all the negative stereotypes of lesbians."

What the hell were they talking about? I didn't write anything like that. Nobody got done at all in my story. I fumbled through my own copy, desperate to find such a passage. This was no orgy. How could they read that into my story? Stereotypes? I thought the stereotype of lesbians was that we were all lonely, desperate and despairing spinsters who, if not completely alone and living at the edge of town, had settled down with high school sweethearts thirty years ago and called each other sister in front of the neighbors. I thought we were all supposed to be sexless, mirthless and hopeless.

Confused, puzzled and hurt, I glanced up at the professor. She was glaring in my direction, her jaw set.

"Let's get one thing perfectly clear," she said, looking away from me. "In this classroom there will be no — and I do mean no — constraints put on the subject matter presented here. I will not allow Melanie or anyone else to be attacked personally." She looked pointedly at each member of the class, ending with me. "Each of you has the inalienable right to write what you write, whatever that is. If you have a personal problem with any given text, you are free to say, 'I may not be the right audience for this piece,' and remain silent. But attempts to silence any voice or to impose your political, religious or pseudomoralistic standards on anyone else's work will not be tolerated. Is that understood?"

Only the white-haired guy spoke. "Well, I certainly did not pay out my good money to come in here and read about lesbian sex."

She spun on her heel, walked slowly to the table he sat at, put both hands on the table and leaned close to his anger-reddened face. In a clear, controlled voice she asked, "Well, where did you want to go to read about lesbian sex?"

The class laughed and the guy got up, gathered his papers and stalked out, slamming the door behind him.

At first the class sat in shocked silence, then the young guy who'd spoken earlier said, "Professor? Aren't you worried that he could make trouble for you?"

"Him? Nah. In the first place, he probably won't do anything but go home and kick his dog. If he does complain, what will he complain about? That I defended a student's First Amendment rights against his unconscionable attack? Good. We could use a little controversy, it's not good to ever feel too safe, too secure. Besides, I have tenure. But let's talk about safety. Melanie's courage in submitting a story she must have known was risky should be an example to us, a reminder that if we risk nothing, we gain nothing. Today . . ."

But I didn't hear another word. I was captivated by the way she moved her left hand through her hair as if it were falling in her eyes. I studied every movement of her hands, her feet, her body, the way she lounged against a table edge, the wall, or slouched in a chair, feet up on another chair, the way she tucked her right thumb into the front pocket of her jeans. A goddess, I decided, the woman is a goddess.

"Professor, are you saying we can write about anything we want — anything?" It was the other likely dyke talking.

"I don't give a turtle's tit what you write about as long as you do it well. And call me Kate, okay? Now let's look at Melanie's story again. What does work and what doesn't — its specific strengths and weaknesses."

And a true, useful critique began. I took copious notes, especially when she summed up.

"My only problem with this piece is that we've got two people in a relationship who are both starting to look around. But why? I'd like some tension built in between these two characters. Is it simply a seven-month itch or do they have deeper problems? See what you can do with that, Mel," she said, handing me her marked-up copy.

The other students filed out, piling their own copies in front of me. I gathered them up and had started to leave when she approached me. She put an arm across my shoulders and gave me a quick squeeze.

"Good show," she said. "I'm glad you're here, Mel. Can I call you Mel? You're a hell of a writer. Thanks for being so open with us."

"That guy . . ."

"Oh, never mind him. There's nothing like a jump start on a semester. This little incident saved us a good month of warm-up time. All the rest of them will open up quicker now. Don't worry about it. I'll see you next week."

She headed for the door, then turned back. "And congratulations on winning the Wickwire fellowship. I was on the committee. I thought you'd like to know it was a unanimous decision." Then she strode out.

Tears trickled down my face as I stood in silent gratitude. A saint, I thought, a goddess and a saint. With a huge grin on my face I walked to the parking lot and crawled into Subie, piling the critiqued copies on the passenger seat. I was eager to get home and go through the comments — especially Kate's. Kate. I could call her Kate. And I would write my heart out for her. I would earn her confidence in me, I would deserve her approval, I promised myself.

But as I neared home, my elation, my determination faded, replaced by the struggle to remember just what it was I needed to get at the hardware store: steel wool, sandpaper, new knobs for the kitchen cupboards. Once home I forgot even to take the stack of copies into the house.

Chapter 7

It was like falling in love, like meeting someone that is so interesting and fun to be with that being with her is everything. Every other relationship or activity fades. For me, school had been my family, my friend, my work and my play. Unlike most of the other students in my classes, I was not going to college for the sole purpose of being more marketable, of being able to earn more money. I loved to study for the sake of study: I loved the intellectual stimulation and the structure. I saw grad school not as an option but a necessity, an excuse to stay in the game I loved and played so well. That's why it now amazes me that my attitude changed so dramatically. But love changes you and blinds you to the changes, until it is too late.

One day I overslept and another I told myself I didn't feel well. Another day the drive seemed formidable. I got to the car door and turned back. And, when I did go, I sat in silence making thumbnail sketches of the professors and my classmates instead of taking notes. Or I'd make lists of supplies for the house.

I'd need more dust masks, a wider brush, turpentine or paint thinner. It was time to start the floors.

As I accumulated more stuff for the house, I piled it on the porch, in anticipation of doing the floors. I couldn't put it off forever, the unseasonably warm weather wouldn't last.

That's one thing about Michigan you can accurately predict: the unpredictability of the weather. Autumn was nowhere in sight except for a few nights when the temperature dipped low enough to turn a few fainthearted young sugar maples bright scarlet. Late September continued not just warm but unseasonably hot, breaking all previous records — one of Michigan's favorite pastimes. "Normal temperatures" has no meaning in Michigan. We've had snow in May, hail in July, tree buds on Valentine's Day and shirtsleeve weather into December. Anything is possible here, and nothing is probable.

At yard sales I'd picked up a vacuum cleaner for five dollars that only needed a new belt, and a set of bunk beds which I separated and placed in each of the upstairs bedrooms. Finally I had a place for Ford to sleep if I could convince her to take off a whole weekend from work. Even an overnighter would be nice. I missed her like crazy.

I'd called the phone company for a hook-up, but the $150 deposit and the $80 installation fee intimidated me. Telling them I'd call back, I checked the dwindling balance in my checkbook. My initial budget had not included the cost of home repairs and some mornings Subie was slow to start, what if she needed work? I decided to put off the phone until the next fellowship disbursement. Surprisingly, it was only when I'd get an urge to talk to Ford that I felt deprived. I certainly didn't miss the endless phone solicitations or the wrong numbers which always seem to come when the perfect phrase or image has just occurred, or when I've finally fallen asleep.

Although I was continually drawn to the downstairs bedroom, which I began to think of as the green room, I was simultaneously repelled by it. After moving my futon into that room, I found it impossible to sleep there. So I'd moved the pad upstairs to the back bedroom which felt neutral, in which I could relax. After I acquired the bunk beds, I moved the futon back downstairs into the green room for which I still could not invent a use.

I bought straw hats whenever I found them and hung them with push pins in a growing cluster on the far wall of the dining room. At one sale I found a woven pink horse blanket, frayed at the edges, that I hung in the doorway between the living room and the green room.

Sometimes I was compelled to go there, to pull

the pink blanket aside and stand looking into the northwest corner but I could not imagine why. I lay the futon there, first north-south, then east-west which seemed right. Sometimes I would lie down there, on my stomach with my right arm out as if someone were beside me, a woman who smelled like flowers.

But even then, I couldn't stay in the room long; a restlessness filled me. I had to get the house ready. But for what? For whom?

Although the weather held, I knew it wouldn't last forever. The floors wanted refinishing. The bedroom — the green room — had the same wood floors, but the finish there was still good. It was clear that others had avoided that room too.

So one morning I moved what little furniture I had into the green room and, dust mask securely in place, I began to sand the floors.

I didn't want to spend the money to rent an industrial floor sander and doubted I could control it anyway. All I had was my small finish sander, so, square foot by square foot, I sanded the floors by hand. With my purple bandanna around my brow, safety glasses and dust mask, I felt pretty *macha* as I roughed up the wood. Taking the previous finish off to the bare wood was beyond my sander's capability but I wanted the polyurethane to take, so I made sure that the few remaining shiny places were dulled and the wood evened out. Occasionally I'd hit a nail or splatter of old paint or something like tar, even a few spots of antiqued chewing gum, so I hammered or scraped or pried as I went. Changing the sandpaper often irritated me, and made me wish I'd popped for the rental, but my physical expenditure seemed important, almost like a requirement.

The work took most of the daylight hours. My knees and back ached and even with the mask my nose felt packed and my tongue grainy.

After a careful vacuuming of the rooms I showered until the hot water ran out. I was tired and achy but pleased with my progress. And I couldn't stop. I mopped the floor with bleach water to take up any of the dust the vacuum missed. This way, I thought, it would be thoroughly dry by morning and I could start the polyurethane first thing.

In clean shorts and T-shirt, I took a jar of tea out onto the porch steps and watched the willow branches sway. The sun was setting, sinking orangely into the far end of US-12, and some small part of me wanted to go too, wanted to drive to meet it right there where the horizon halved it, then quartered it, then slivered it. That small part of me longed to be where it was warm all year round, where people own houses, not the other way around.

With a guilty start, I looked behind me, as if the house could hear my disloyal thoughts. What a terrible thing to think, what an irrational, traitorous thought. Never mind, I told myself, I'd make it up to her. I'd repair the damage. That very night. I'd put the finish on.

I went back in and, again on my hands and knees, applied an even coat of polyurethane to the floors — four-inch square by four-inch square, first stroke against the grain, the second stroke with it. Slowly, deliberately, I worked, with no thought in my mind other than how it would look when completed and what project I would start next and how I would accomplish it. I didn't even think about where I'd sleep; I'd sealed the area, with no access to my bedroom.

So I cleaned my brush, my hands and legs, closed the nearly empty can and slept in Subie. Thankfully, my afghanomaniac grandmother had made one to match my car.

It was after two.

I'd intended to sand again, do two coats. But when I went inside the next morning, stiff from my labor and from Subie's unyielding bed, I changed my mind. It was beautiful, rich, gleaming. And I'd done it. Overlaying the chemical fumes was the smell of flowers, sweet and intoxicating. It was worth it.

Then I realized my mistake. Doing the floor first meant I'd have to be more careful with later projects, the plastering for instance. I'd have to use drop cloths to protect what I'd done. But I didn't care.

Seeing the floors gleam gave me the impetus to do more. What about that stairwell? It'd become a habit as I went up or down the stairs to peel off another swatch of old wallpaper which came off willingly enough. I thought it would not take long.

So I began that project in earnest.

In some places the layered papers came off in huge barklike chunks, in others they clung tightly at one print or another and I would soak them down with water from a spray bottle. At one point I looked up the stairs and saw glimpses of all the papers at once, like looking at patches of the house's history. Someone — who? — thought for some reason — what? — that this paper or that one looked nice here, added something — why?

I counted eight layers of wallpaper, each laid over the others and all different. There was the pink beribboned one, the deep red one with dark geometric shapes, a dark green one with peacocks, and so on down to a layer of newspaper before the plaster and lath wall itself. What was the newspaper for, I wondered. Was it decorative or used for some practical purpose, like sizing, maybe? Someday I'd research this, I thought. And what about the wallpapers themselves? If they could tell the stories of the people who'd hung them, what would they say?

Personally, I preferred the bare white of the highly textured plaster. In several places it was broken away from the lath. I knew I should, probably would, patch this plaster too. But I liked seeing the lath, exposed here and there like ribs, a reminder that beneath prettiness was structure.

Then I began to think of the lath like ribs, the plaster like flesh, the wallpapers like layers of skin. I shook myself, the image was creepy. Houses aren't living things. Even when they're built of things that were once alive — like the logs, the beams, the floorboards, the lathwork — they are not alive. They are not alive.

Chapter 8

"I still wish I'd gone to barber college," I told Ford as I gave her a trim on my porch.

"It's not too late."

"I'm too damn allergic. But I did visit one, though."

"No shit. When? Why didn't you tell me?"

"I don't know, I guess I felt like a failure or something. It was last spring, before I found out about the fellowship. I went to the one in Lansing, filled out the forms, took the entrance exam, took the tour. But by then I knew I couldn't do it. I could barely stand to be in the building, even, with the perm lotion, sprays, dyes. God, it was awful. I told them about it. They said they could maybe work around it for teaching technique — using water instead of lotion for perms — but when I took my licensing exam I'd have to use the real thing. So I had to back out of it."

"That's too bad, babe, I know you're a fiend for cutting hair."

"Yeah. And that's all I wanted to do — cut hair. But you can't get licensed just for that."

"So here you are, still just doing it for love."

"Doing it for food."

I'd called Ford earlier that day from the corner bar on my way home from my feminist lit class. It had been over a month since her last visit.

"I've started talking to myself, Ford," I pleaded. "I need company."

"And I need a trim."

We'd wolfed down the barely warm, foil-wrapped tacos she'd brought from El Chapulin in Adrian. They make the best Mexican food in Lenawee county now that the health department closed down Rosalinda's. In Saginaw, the best is at La Placita which Ford always calls La Placenta.

She always knows where the best Mexican food is; within minutes of entering a new city, she'll have found the place that makes their own tortillas, boils their own beans and uses just the right proportion of cumin in their rice. Once I suggested we collaborate on a dining guide to the Best Michigan Mexican Meals. But she said it'd never sell — just get stolen.

I'm uncomfortable when she makes these kinds of remarks, and I've tried to call her on them. But she tells me she has an ethnic right, being half Mexican on her mother's side.

When her folks first met, her dad could not speak Spanish and her mother could not speak English. They met when she flew up to Adrian to stay with her uncle who was a friend of Ford's dad. She came to study English in hopes of becoming a translator back home in Mexico and the family decided the best way to learn "good" English was to become steeped in it. The language barrier didn't stop them from falling in love. Each worked hard to learn the other's native tongue, but they worked even harder at other things, which is why when Ford was born her mother still spoke little English.

When a "gray lady" — a hospital auxiliary volunteer — came to help her fill out the birth registration form, Ford's mother had just opened a long-awaited letter she'd received from her sister Elizabetta. Now, as Ford tells this story, this gray lady was about ninety and couldn't hear so well. She couldn't speak Spanish at all and could not understand why anyone would want to. So when she tried to find out what name to put on the form, Mrs. Ford thought she was asking about the letter, and answered, *"Mi hermana Elizabetta."*

So the gray lady wrote down Hermana Elizabetta Ford, carefully asking how to spell each word. When Ford's dad got there that evening, he learned of the mistake and, in his broken Spanish, told his wife. She thought it was so funny they never changed it. So my best friend is named Sister Elizabeth.

"I should've been a nun," she says, "but I was raised Lutheran, which eliminated that option. So I just grew up lesbian, which is even better."

We met in college, became instant friends while standing in line to register for classes and making jokes about majoring in "wimmin's" studies and minoring in softball.

Ford's folks had agreed to pay for all her college expenses if she would continue to manage their golf course for five years after she graduated. She'd worked there every chance she got since she was twelve — after school, weekends, summers. By the time she was sixteen she was managing the place and her folks were developing an adjoining apartment complex where the units could be rented by the week, month, or year, with rental rates lower for longer leases. As they had done with the golf course, they were developing the complex in stages, personally supervising each detail.

Fortunately, Ford didn't have to major in business if she didn't want to. She could pursue any field of study that appealed to her. So she changed her major three times, her minor twice, and graduated with a degree in philosophy.

"There is a direct link between philosophy and golf," she claims. "I putt, therefore I am."

As it happened, Ford's parents were the ones who told her she was a lesbian.

At thirteen, she hadn't once begged to have a boy-girl party, wear makeup, or be allowed to date. She virtually lived at the golf course, working or playing, even coaching beginners. Her father could put down practically any piece of equipment or paperwork and Ford could pick it up and operate or process it.

So one day when she got home, her parents were sitting at the kitchen table waiting for her.

"Ford," her father said, calling her by their last name, as he always did, "your mother and I want to talk to you."

"Need to," corrected her mother. "We need to talk to you."

Since they were holding hands across the table, Ford figured it was serious. Ordinarily, each of her parents was strong enough to handle just about anything alone. She poured herself a glass of milk and sat across from them, waiting.

They looked at each other, then her father began, "Ford, we want to ... need to ... talk to you about ... becoming a woman, about what kind of woman you are going to be ..."

"Pops, I know all about periods. I've been having them for three years, remember? And I'm never going to shave my legs."

"No, honey, this is about —"

"Oh, I get it. The birds and the bees. Come on, you guys, I know all that stuff."

Ford's mother took over. "Hermana, listen to us. We are your parents and we love you. We don't want you to waste a lot of time and energy working this out a hard way. Maybe we're supposed to but we don't want to watch you struggle harder than you have to and maybe hurt people or do things you don't have to do. Life is hard enough. Love is even harder. Now listen to me. Those birds and bees — sometimes there are girl birds that only want to be with girl birds. Boy birds, too, sometimes only want to be with boy birds. Bees, too. Everywhere, every kind of specials —"

"Species," corrected Ford's father.

"Whatever. You are one of those kinds of birds so

don't bother trying to be one of the other kinds. Okay?"

Ford had looked at each of her parents' concerned faces, finished her milk, shrugged and said, "Okay."

I finished her trim and she swept up the clippings as I put my kit away. She was regaling me with stories from work.

"There's this woman — a regular — one of the top flakes of the Adrian upper crust. At least as far as money goes. But she has the breeding of a warthog and the libido of a mink. Anyway, she decides she wants to play hide the kielbasa with her golf partner who just happens to be her husband's business partner. So she climbs across him as he sits in the golf cart parked out in that big stand of trees over by the sand trap. So they're busy making a hole in one when suddenly she thinks she sees her husband at the next green. She panics and her vagina spasms and the guy can't get out. The harder they try, the worse she panics and the tighter she gets. Fortunately, Doc Kenefic is in the bar when they come in on the cart, and he gives her a shot of Valium so she can relax. Problem is, she's been screwing him too, and I really have to work to convince him to help her. He wanted to go call her husband and invite him out for a few rounds."

"Ford," I said, fighting a laugh, "is that the truth?"

"Mel, baby, would I ever lie to you?"

"God, Ford, you're too much. Let's go in, it's getting chilly."

So we went in and sat for a while at my new table and chairs that Mrs. Belmont sent out with Ford, along with the fold-out couch, a floor lamp and an apple pie.

"The furniture is really nice, Ford. Are you sure Mrs. B isn't using it?"

"Absolutely. It was stored in that big old garage of hers. She told me it had belonged to one of her husbands."

"One of her husbands? How many has she had?"

"Oh, I don't know, four or five."

"Geez, maybe she is one of us. You know what they say about a lot of husbands being just the flip side of none."

"Yeah, well, the pie convinced me. She never made me any damn pie. She told me that every time she'd get married again, she'd go over the guy's stuff and whatever was the best quality she'd keep in the house and the rest she'd put out in the garage."

"Upgrading, huh?"

"I guess. By the way, she said to ask you if you need any rugs, which anyone could see you do. She's got some nice hand-knotted, hand-cut area rugs she said you could have."

"What am I going to have to do to pay for all this stuff?"

"Well, hell, Mel, she's just one little old lady. It can't take much."

I threw an ice cube at her.

* * * * *

57

"Well, Mel, what's up with you? I'm glad you called — I might've forgotten to take a day off this week — but you seem, I don't know, subdued."

I shrugged. "No, I'm fine. Really. I'm just . . . I've been working hard lately and . . ."

"New story? What's it about? Me?" She mugged for me, earning half a smile.

"No. No, actually, I meant on the house. Fixing it up."

"Well, so what about school? How's it going?"

"Oh, fine, fine. I'm . . . it's fine."

"So tell me about it. Meet any babes?"

"No, Ford. No babes. Besides, I thought you just met someone new."

"Where'd you hear that?"

"Ford." I tried to look reproving, "You have always just met someone new."

"Oh, yeah, I forgot."

"Okay, so when do I get to meet her? What's her name? Have you done her yet?"

"Mel, I am appalled. How can you even ask me that?"

"So you haven't."

"Haven't what?"

"Haven't done her yet."

"How do you know that?"

"Because if you had, you'd have admitted it. You tell me everything you do and nothing you don't."

"I do?"

"Always."

"Maybe you know me too well."

"So, when do I get to meet Tinalisajill?"

"Who?"

"Your new girlfriend."

58

"What did you call her?"

"Tinalisajill. All your girlfriends are called either Tina or Lisa or Jill. Haven't you ever noticed that?"

"They are not. What about Kathy? Or Robin?"

"Name two more."

"Get me some more iced tea."

"Get your own damned iced tea."

"Hey, I'm company."

"You are not company, you are family. Get it yourself."

She rose, jar in hand.

"Oh, and Ford? While you're up?"

"What?"

I handed her my jar. "Get me some, too."

She grumbled untranslatable growls and snarls, but brought us each a fresh jarful. I knew she would.

"So what do you think it means?" Ford picked a hair clipping out of her jar and wiped it on her jeans.

"What do I think what means?"

"You know, that I date a lot of Tinas, Lisas and Jills?" She looked like she might be heading into a serious pondering of this question.

"Well, I think it means that twenty-odd years ago a lot of new moms were naming their daughters Tina, Lisa or Jill. That's all."

She looked hopeful. "Whew. What a relief. I was afraid it was something Freudian."

"Karmic, maybe."

"Something. Listen, speaking of girlfriends . . ."

"Yes, speaking of girlfriends, when do I get to meet her?"

"Well, not yet. We're not at that stage yet. I'm

still trying to convince her I'm irresistible. Meeting my crazy writer friend could scare her off."

"Afraid she'll like me better?"

"No way. I think she has a fixation for employed persons."

"Gee thanks, Ford."

"Hey, Mel, you're a writer. People don't expect the same things from artistic types. You're supposed to be erratic, withdrawn, isolated. Hey, maybe that's why you wanted to move out here all alone and be antisocial."

"I am not antisocial. I am ... private. And besides, I feel like I'm never alone."

"What do you mean by that, Mel? You are totally alone. It's creepy."

Remembering our last conversation, I hesitated to go on, but needed to, had to. "Ford, it's what we talked about before. It's this house. Maybe it is what you said — haunted."

"Oh, shit. Here we go again. Next you're going to tell me you've got a ghost. Right. So what's her sign? I assume it's a she."

I ignored her sarcasm. "Ford, I'm serious. This place is strange. Maybe the house *does* have a ghost — something. There's some kind of presence, and I feel like we're connected somehow. Like it ... no, she ... it is a she ... cares for me. She likes it when I ..."

Ford looked really worried at this point and I didn't blame her. "Mel —"

"No, wait. I know. I know it sounds crazy. But hear me out. While I'm working on the house, it feels like she watches me. It's almost as if she ... encourages me. I almost think ... Oh, never mind." I shook my head, tears of frustration gathering. How could I make her understand what I didn't?

For a while she was silent, then said, "Go on, Mel. I'm listening. Tell me."

I looked at her and saw, not interest or encouragement, but resignation on her face. It was enough. It was enough that she was willing to listen.

"The perfume, Ford. You smelled it. Flowers. I smell it almost all the time — often. And you know how allergic I am. You know I can't be around most perfumes. They wipe me out, incapacitate me. But look at me. I don't know when I've felt stronger, more energetic. Even when the perfume is the strongest, I can breathe. And I love it. I almost need it. It's like an addiction. And it isn't just the perfume. It's ... temperature. Sometimes it gets warm, as if she approves of what I'm doing, of me. But sometimes it gets so damn cold as if she doesn't. The other day, I was reading my Becca poems aloud and the room got so cold. And sometimes —"

"You were reading poems to a ghost?"

"No! Of course not! I just felt like reading them, I read all my work that way. But listen, this is the best part —"

"Best part, Mel? Best? None of this is good."

"It doesn't get better. I think she ... puts ideas in my head." I waited for the explosive reaction I anticipated, but Ford just looked at me blankly. "I think she tells me what she wants done with the house, how she wants it fixed up or changed. And she tells me where I leave things ..." I trailed off, realizing what I'd think if it were Ford telling me these things.

Ford was silent.

"Oh," I said, "I know it sounds nuts. Maybe I am nuts, but you smelled the perfume too."

"It could have come from outside somewhere."

"It didn't."

Ford got up and got another jar of tea. She walked with it around the two rooms, looking at my pictures, the driftwood, out the front door, then back to my desk.

"You left your typewriter on," she said, switching Rosa off.

"Yeah. I forgot again. I was working on something and walked away."

"You'll waste electricity."

"Don't turn into my father," I warned her. "If you start nagging me, I'll have to leave it on all the time in protest. It costs pennies to run her, maybe nickels. But even if it's dimes, they are my damn dimes."

"You were working on something? What? A duty roster?"

I half smiled. At least when she's being sarcastic she isn't being silent.

"No," I said. "A poem."

She looked at me, lifted one eyebrow. Then she resumed her prowl, looking again at all the things she'd already seen.

Finally she said, "Did I ever tell you about my friend Val? From high school? She was always kind of flaky, but she's really into, um, spiritual stuff. Maybe I could bring her out here sometime? You know, see what she thinks?"

I could've hugged her. I was so grateful for her change of heart. "So you do believe me?"

She looked at me and shook her head. "I don't know what I believe, but I do know you. You get a little crazy sometimes, but you're not crazy. If you say something is here, then something is here. Let's find out what."

Chapter 9

A yard sale gave me a chance to explore my new
hometown. Orange fluorescent signs announcing
Cement City's First Annual Garage Sale lured me
past my driveway, down Cement City Highway and
across the new Goose Creek bridge. A rusted
"Business District" sign was partially obscured by yet
another orange sign pointing left into the heart of
the community.

On the left were the village offices, housed in
what had once been the train depot. Clearly, no
trains had gone through Cement City in many years;

even the rails and wood ties had been taken up. The depot was painted Wedgewood blue with white trim.

A few doors down there was a brick post office and, in the next block, a gas station-garage, corner grocery store and ramshackle bar. Everything, in fact, except the starkly neat post office, needed paint or siding or a good scrubdown. Here and there someone had obviously tried to dress up the village: a few stoic marigolds squatted in a planter outside the gas station, a litter barrel with a lion's head lid.

I parked off the road near the post office and went to examine the many displays of dusty, unwanted used items. Sometimes the least promising sales yield the best finds.

The residents seemed listless and suspicious of the few customers their First Annual Yard Sale attracted. Working my way up and down the main street, where most of the sales were set up on card, picnic and kitchen tables and the ground, I picked up a half-dead split-leaf philodendron I thought I could resuscitate, several candles for my ongoing collection, one sterling silver fork and a delicate glass bowl with a ruffled neck. It was just the thing for the rose petals I'd picked off the semi-wild bush growing in the front yard and had spread to dry on newspapers on my kitchen counters. I bought a badly handmade blue pottery pitcher for my desk top, for pens or maybe as a vase for wildflowers.

As I browsed, I tried to make small talk with the surly-looking merchants-for-a-day, but with no success.

"Hi, how are you?" met with a suspicious glare.

"Beautiful weather, isn't it?" met with a sullen nod but averted eyes.

"What can you tell me about your town?" I asked one woman who froze in the middle of making change for another customer.

It was the customer who answered, but first with a question.

"You're not from around here, are you?"

I shook my head.

She was short, white-haired, round, and had the brightest blue eyes I'd ever seen, and the quickest smile. We walked together for a little bit.

"I don't live here either, not right here, I mean. I live about seven miles in that direction." She pointed one way and then paused, rethinking, then pointed in another direction. "Or maybe that way." Then she laughed. "Oh well, I can get home when I want to. But let's see, you were asking about Cement City. I can tell you a little bit. Actually, I don't know how it survives. Pure stubbornness, I guess. Years and years ago it was quite prosperous, I understand. There were seven banks in town."

"Seven banks? I don't think there are seven blocks."

"That's probably about right, one on every block. It was the cement plant that brought in the money. Everybody in town worked there."

"Or the banks."

She laughed and nodded. "Then it all came to an end. Not suddenly, not just like that." She snapped her fingers. "It just died out gradually. I don't recall just why. Economic fluctuations, mismanagement, shortsightedness. Maybe a war or two. You know, the usual things that kill small towns."

"Only Cement City didn't die."

"No. No, it didn't. Every once and a while, though, someone moves in and tries to create some interest here. Usually the first thing they do is try to change the name ..."

"Oh, no. It's a wonderful name. I'll bet it's the only one in the country."

"Well, the old ones, the ones that still remember how it was, fight them down. Maybe when they're gone someone will succeed."

"Oh, I hope not."

She smiled at me and patted my arm maternally. "Me too. It isn't a pretty name but it's ... rich. Textured, you know. Oh, and let's see, I don't know his name or even if the story's true, but there's supposed to be a man here with a bad limp who was caught in the gunfire of an escaping gang of bank robbers. Hmmm. Did I hear it was Al Capone? Did he rob banks? Oh well, it was someone famous, anyway."

"What a great story."

"Isn't it? Don't you just love stories like that?"

I nodded. "Listen," I said, "do you know if there's a book about Cement City somewhere? Its history?"

"Oh, not really, I don't think so. But in a room of the old depot — it's the village offices now — they tried to set up an archive." She pointed it out to me. "It's not much, but I'm glad they tried. You should go look around if you're interested."

"I think I will, thanks. Thanks so much." I offered her my hand but she unexpectedly hugged me.

"I'm so glad to meet a young person who's interested in old things. I wish someone would ...

Well, never mind. Perhaps we'll meet again. That would be nice. I like you. What did you say your name was?"

"Melanie. Melanie Myer."

"Melanie. Melanie. I must remember that. Bye-bye now."

She got into a nearby rose-colored Prizm, executed a U-turn and drove off down a side street in the direction she had first pointed.

She was right about the archive. It was disappointing. One room held a few front pages of the local newspaper mounted behind Plexiglass sheets, a train lantern, some photographs of somber men in somber clothes, and a few sheets of handwritten accounts from the first telephone company. The focus was clearly on the trains, the cement plant, and the depot itself. Nothing about the people, nothing of the house on the hill, which was probably an unremarkable log outbuilding at the time.

I stopped at the store for a loaf of bread and a bottle of Pepsi and then went home.

Chapter 10

"Dear Melanie," the letter began.

I knew it was from my mom before I opened it. It was handwritten, barely legible. My mom is one of the people the post office administrators had in mind when they made the regulations about letters being addressed in print, all caps.

She always calls me Melanie; a nickname would be too familiar, would imply some closeness, and there's no point in deceiving ourselves about these things, is there?

My dad calls me Sis which I've always liked but

never understood. He types his letters to me and, beyond the informal nickname, his letters are almost as impersonal as hers. He does, however, occasionally ask questions about my life, questions like "Is your Subaru still running?" and "Do you like graduate school?" Simple, direct, yes-or-no questions. Nothing, ever, to suggest more than surface interest in my life.

"Your father and I are very busy," I decipher, wondering why I bother. I could just memorize one letter and recite it to myself every month or so. Save her the postage.

They love Florida, there's lots to do. Everything is more expensive than they'd planned so they can't offer me any help right now (as if I've asked them to). She has some health concerns. He has a new part-time job. On Friday (or Saturday) they are going to dinner with her sister/niece/cousin/friends.

My father, like me, is an only child, so it's my mother's relatives that provide family ties. Somehow I always seem to get factored out of the family equation, which is mostly fine with me. They usually treat me like some exotic, colorful, but possibly dangerous insect. To me, they seem like drab domestic, and most assuredly dangerous insects.

Except my father who occasionally displays traits similar to mine.

Like me, my father has an insatiable curiosity about the world, about things in it, how they operate, how to make them or how to fix them. On one Saturday before they moved, he and I had sprawled in front of the television watching one PBS program after another: Cajun cooking, French cooking, cooking cheap and healthy, installing track lighting, installing ceramic tile. It was our version of quality time: hours and hours of endless information. Finally my mom came in and said, "Well, I'm sick and tired of being educated, I want to be entertained. Turn the station."

So he did, to a game show of some kind.

"See, " she said, "this is educational too."

Neither of us protested, resisted or refused. But it was like looking at a tiny pile of crushed powder where an opal had been.

I haven't come out to them — not in any official, formal way. Not that I haven't tried, at least, to broach the topic. Sometimes I think they know but don't know they know; sometimes I think they know for sure but absolutely do not wish to discuss it. Other times I think they don't have a clue.

Occasionally I've tried to ease into the subject. Once I was putting on my socks and shoes in the living room. My dad was in there, too. I realized that the sock I'd already put on was inside out so, instead of taking it off and righting it, I turned the other one inside out too and put it on.

"Geez, Mel," I said out loud to myself, "that was a queer thing to do."

My dad said quietly, "Sis, do you do queer things?"

It was my opening, my chance, for which I'd lived half-poised. I jumped at it. Keeping my eyes on my shoes as I put them on, I said, "Yes, Daddy, I do. I just never knew how to tell you." Then I held my breath, not knowing what to expect.

He laughed. Laughed and laughed and laughed.

Then there was the time when, in a restaurant with my folks and one of Mom's cousins, I made some mildly disparaging remark about men.

"Why, Melanie," the cousin said. "Do you hate men?"

"No," I answered. "I don't hate men. Why should I? I don't have to sleep with them."

There was a quarter-beat of silence. Then they all laughed. *Oh, Melanie, Melanie, Melanie, you are such a stitch.*

Another time my mom was talking about some nephew whose girlfriend was pregnant.

"Jason?" I said, "That's a surprise. I thought he walked on the other side of the street."

"Oh, I never thought that," she said, never looking up from her knitting. She didn't even ask what I meant by that, and maybe I'm naive, but it surprised me that she knew what I was saying. Maybe it was the context. But then, she does watch a lot of Oprah.

When a professor in my freshman year brought me a T-shirt from her trip to Paris, I explained that she and I were good friends. My mom had looked at the shirt, then at me, then back at the shirt. Then she gave me that over-the-top-of-her-glasses look and said, "Well, it seems like more than that to me." Neither of us pursued it.

Eventually I gave up trying to tell them something they didn't want to hear. I think that's why their letters are so generic — we have an unspoken contract. If they don't ask me specifics about my life, I won't tell them.

Except for my dad, I've often felt like an alien around my family anyway; being lesbian just compounds it. Maybe someone forgot to give me my make- nice-pill. They act as if, at any given moment, without warning, I might say something awful, like the truth about what I think or feel, which would, of course, be unforgivable, a disaster. Etiquette beats honesty and outward appearances beat truth in our family and silence keeps you in the game. Their silences and the silence expected of me is what drove me to write. Sent to my room for yet another impertinence, I would scribble out an alternative ending to the episode. Sometimes I would simply write them all off the face of the earth. But often, in these stories, I would be the one to whom they turned for advice or guidance; occasionally they would suddenly realize that I was right and they would thank and praise me. Those were the earliest stories. Later I would write all our ugly secrets matter-of-factly, as if there were nothing odd about our family's carefully tended lies.

What if, instead, they started to tell their own truths about their thoughts and feelings?

What if my cousin Anita sobered up long enough to speak her pain over having her father take those nude photographs of her in her early teens? What if her mother sobered up enough to speak the pain of her betrayal by her husband? What if he sobered up enough to explain what those photo sessions really meant to him?

"Well, they were very artistically done," my mother told me.

"Then why aren't they displayed proudly? Entered in art shows? Why doesn't anyone do more than whisper the story of their existence?"

"Melanie, that's enough."

73

But it's not enough for me, it's never been enough, as far back as I can remember.

At 14.

"Why doesn't anyone tell Aunt Lynn she has emphysema so she can quit smoking and live longer?"

"The doctor didn't think we should."

"Why?"

"Because she's old. It would be too hard for her to quit."

"But she's important. And it's her body, her life. She has a right to know."

"Melanie, that's enough."

At 12.

"Why does Uncle Jack always walk in on me when I'm in the bathroom?"

"He probably didn't know you were in there."

"Yes, he did. He watched me."

"Well, he just made a mistake."

"Every time we go over there?"

"Melanie, that's enough."

At 6.

"Why do you get up a half hour before Daddy to put on your makeup?"

"Because I want to look nice for him."

"Doesn't he like how you look in just your face?"

"Melanie . . ."

* * * * *

At 4.

"Bedtime, Melanie. Come on, Mommy will read you a nice story."

"No. I don't want a nice story. I want Daddy to tell me something real."

"Okay, Sis, here I am. Let's see ... did you know that in Panama there is a plant that grows at the bases of trees and climbs them? Its flower is as big as a dinner plate and has such a strong fragrance that you can smell it from a quarter of a mile away. It takes six weeks for the bud to form, but it only blossoms for one night. It's called a night blooming cereus."

"Serious? Like, I'm serious?"

"No. C-e-r-e-u-s. And once you smell it you never forget it, never ever ever."

Chapter 11

"Mel, this is my friend Val. Val, this is my friend Mel," Ford said.

I said, "What? No gold loop earrings?"

"They're at the cleaners," Val said, "with the turban and cape."

"And the diaphanous full skirts of mysteriously changing colors?" I smiled.

"Sorry to disappoint you. Just jeans and a T-shirt," she said.

"Which, I might add, fit you very well indeed."

If I'd dreaded meeting Ford's "flaky" friend, or

had preconceived notions of what she would look or act like, one glance dispelled them all. She was tall and relaxed, dark-haired, green-eyed and cheerful. All of which switched me on to automatic flirt.

"Yeah, yeah, yeah," said Ford, "she ain't too bad for a straight white girl."

"Straight?"

Val lifted her shoulders in a prolonged shrug, hands up and out. "Yeah, well, what can you do?"

I put one arm around her and led her into the dining room. "So, tell me, Val," I said, "just what is it you people want anyway?"

"Oh, leave her alone," grouched Ford.

But Val was laughing. She was also looking around the room.

"Ford tells me you're at Adrian. I heard about their new graduate program. You're the first class, aren't you?"

I nodded. "Pioneers."

Val laughed. "I'd like to read your work sometime."

"So would I," I joked. "And pretty damn soon."

"Can't you write here?"

"I never thought it mattered where I was. I've written in the car, in the park, on planes, on vacations, anywhere day or night. So I can't figure out why I'm not writing. I'm even relatively happy here, now. But . . . nothing. Well, my journal occasionally. Not like before. Every time I think maybe I'll work on something I end up working on the house instead and never get around to any serious writing."

Again she scanned the rooms, then looked at me. "I feel it. I can feel the presence here."

"I told her what you told me, Mel," Ford said. She turned to Val. "So whadaya think, Doc? Can you make it go away?"

"Go away?" I was instantly outraged. "I don't want her to go away. I never said that. Ford, what are you trying to do?"

"I thought we were going to drive it away. I thought — "

"Well, you thought wrong." I turned from Ford and looked into Val's green eyes. "Look, I only want to know who she is, what she wants. I want to understand. This is not — I repeat, not — about driving her off."

It was the first time in our five-year friendship that I'd raised my voice to Ford. She looked as stunned as I felt.

Val spoke. "Good. I'm glad. That's not what I came for anyway. Walk with me through the house. Talk to me as we go, about anything, about the house or yourself, anything. Not questions, though, just talk."

First I went to Ford, put a hand on her arm. "I'm sorry I snapped at you. I didn't meant to do that."

She looked hurt and confused. "That's not like you, Mel. I've never heard you . . . well, except for that one time when that guy cut you off on the expressway and you followed him all the way home and told him off right there in his own front yard."

"Ford, that was you. I was the one cowering in your passenger seat."

"Oh, that's right," she said, smiling at last.

I hugged her then, understanding I'd been forgiven.

Then she said, "Hey, Mrs. B sent your rugs. I'll unload them."

"If you wait a minute, I'll help," I offered.

"Help? Help? Dykes don' need no stinking help," she drawled, making muscles and posing in absurd positions.

As Ford unloaded, I led Val slowly through the house. Recounting what little I knew of its history, I showed her the beams in the living room, the green room, the upstairs bedrooms, the basement with its unpeeled logs. In each room we'd pause and she would just stand and breathe, slowly, deeply, then she'd indicate with a nod or an arm movement that she was ready to move on.

There were three rolls of rugs waiting when we returned to the dining room.

"Where do you want them?" Ford asked.

"I can do that later," I said.

"Mel, would you for crying out loud let a person do a thing? I'm feeling like an idiot here. Let me do this."

I hated to interrupt our exploration, but Val smiled and nodded.

"Okay," I said, "Let's have a look at them." But I already knew from their undersides what colors they were and where they belonged: the peach one in the dining room, the black one in the living room, and the green one, naturally, in the green room with the philodendron, which was already sending up new growth. Still we unrolled them.

"Holy shit," was Val's not very mystical response. "These are gorgeous. Where did you get them?"

Ford told her. I couldn't. I was on my knees, running my hands over the rich colors, patterns, textures.

"My landlady's got a crush on Mel. She gave these to her."

"Gave? Did you say gave?"

"Yup."

"Lucky woman. These are lovely."

Finally I found my voice again. "Too bad she's about a hundred and ten. Please thank her for me, Ford. No. Never mind. I'll write to her. This just astounds me."

"Well, where do you want them?"

Val answered, "The green one in that front bedroom, the black one in the living room and the peach one in here."

Then she looked at me, startled. "I'm sorry. That's none of my business."

"It's okay," I assured her. "That's exactly where I want them."

Ford busied herself distributing the rugs, moving the furniture out of the way, then replacing it. I only interrupted to tell her to put the living room one down on a diagonal. Then Val and I settled on the couch as Ford went to get some tea.

"Well, what do you think?" I asked, eager for her opinion.

She sighed, "Well, you've got something here, all right."

"I wish you could smell the perfume. Some kind of flowers."

"Maybe I will when she manifests."

"Did you say 'she'?"

"Oh, yes, definitely she. Definitely female, feminine. You are absolutely right about that. And what was it your landlady said about women being uncomfortable here?"

"Just that. She said she'd feel better if I were a man. I thought she was being sexist, or even homophobic."

"Probably not. Your . . . entity probably doesn't manifest to men. Hmmm . . . that's interesting. She could be lesbian, too."

"Cool. That explains so much. Sometimes I feel like she's . . . flirting with me."

"I sense you feel affection for this presence."

I hesitated. I hadn't thought about it.

"Yes," I said, "I feel . . . blessed. Sort of. Is that too corny a word?"

"Not if that's how you feel."

"I've never felt . . . particularly . . . what? Special. Not even acceptable. I've always felt I was odd — at least to my family."

"*Queer* is a better word for you," said Ford, setting down three jars of tea and joining us on the couch. "You need a chair or two in here. What would you like? I'll tell Mrs. B."

"Mel, a lot of people seem to think you're pretty special. I do and I've only just met you. Mrs. B obviously does and Ford here thinks the sun rises so you can write about it."

"Yes, I know. I have the most incredible luck with friends. My friends are the finest people I know. But I'm less lucky with family and with lovers — girlfriends. But now this — you called her an entity? She makes me feel special. She makes me feel . . . appreciated. I think she appreciates me, the things I do. I can't . . . imagine . . ."

A heaviness slowly settled against the back of my neck, along my collarbone. My arms suddenly felt so heavy.

"Oh, fuck. Ford? Ford, I have to lie down now. Right now. I'm sorry. I'm so sorry. I haven't had one of these spells in so long. I thought I was well. I thought . . ."

Ford and Val both rose from the couch, leaving me room to stretch out. Ford explained, "She gets like this. Weak. She'll be okay. It's just scary at first. She's got this . . ."

I was struggling to stay alert, to talk, "I hate weakness. I hate that I get like this. It's been so long . . ."

"No," Val said. "Don't fight it. Just relax. Relax, Mel. Breathe. Breathe deeply. Close your eyes. Everything is going to be all right. Give it away."

I could hear her talk to me but her voice became fainter and fainter, as if she were moving away from me, farther and farther away.

"Sam," I heard myself say.

"She's coming around," I heard Val say a while later. It didn't seem like I'd been out for very long.

Propping myself up on an elbow, I shook my head to clear it. "God, that was a strange one."

"Ford? Are you okay?"

Ford was staring at me, mouth and eyes wide open.

"Ford? I'm sorry. Did I scare you? But you've seen me zonk out before. Ford? Talk to me."

But she didn't. I looked at Val for some clue to my friend's behavior.

Tears were streaming down Val's cheeks. "I can't tell you how much this means to me," she said. "Thank you, thank you, thank you."

"For what?"

"Gardenias. The flowers are gardenias. Every Mother's Day my father buys my mother a gardenia plant which she manages to kill by summer. But that's the perfume."

"You smelled it? Oh, I'm glad. Then you met her? She came while I was out?"

Val covered her mouth with both of her hands to stifle a hysterical laugh. "Yes, you could say that. She spoke to me."

"You talked to her?" I asked, sitting up on the couch.

"No. I mean she spoke to me — to us — through you."

"Through me?" I was totally baffled. What was she talking about?

Val nodded, still trying not to laugh. "Yes. Yes, yes, yes, yes, yes, yes. She said . . . Oh God, I wish I'd known this was going to happen. I wish I'd taped this. And I'm supposed to be a sensitive. You must be like a superconductor. God, this is so exciting."

Ford moved then, slightly, enough to look in Val's direction.

Val was still talking, almost babbling. "I was going to suggest automatic writing, hoping for contact that way."

"Automatic writing?"

"Yes, you hold a pencil above a piece of paper, let it dangle actually, and sometimes words appear. The pencil moves and . . . I've seen it done. I thought . . . I can barely believe this."

"I still don't know what the hell you are talking about."

She stopped, looked at me, and shook her head. "Mel. Okay. I'll try to explain. You went into a trance."

"A trance? Me? I went into a trance?"

"Yes. That wasn't one of what you call your 'spells.' Unless . . . no, wait, let's deal with this first. When you . . . zonk, you call it?"

I nodded, "Zonk doesn't sound so . . . invalidish. One of my doctors said to think of it as being born a hundred years too late — or too early. But I hate this weakness of mine."

"Maybe it's not a weakness. Maybe it's a strength. A gift. Maybe . . ."

"Val, what happened to me? Just tell me, please."

"Of course. How do you feel?"

"Fine. The heaviness is gone, the drowsiness. I feel . . . refreshed. Like it never happened."

"Is that how you usually feel after one of your spells?"

"Well, no, not exactly. Usually my strength returns more gradually. Why? And what do you mean by 'trance'?"

Ford, pale, would occasionally switch her gaze from Val to me, but she was still not speaking.

"What's the matter with Ford?" I asked.

"She's . . . I think a good word would be *stunned.* She didn't expect . . . but then, neither did I."

"What? What the hell happened?"

Val was beaming. "Mel, your ghost, she spoke to us through you."

"Spoke?"

"Yes, spoke. With words. Only it wasn't your voice."

It was my turn to stare silently.

"Her voice was softer, more — don't be offended — more feminine. A slight accent, soft slow drawl. Like . . . maybe Southern. Sexy."

"What did she say?"

Val took a deep breath, sighing. "She said 'Leave us alone. I want you to leave us alone. We belong together.' I asked her what she wanted. She said, 'I want only what is mine.' Then I asked — oh, God, you're going to love this — I asked why she can't rest. And she got all haughty and said, 'I beg your pardon but there is nothing wrong with my rest.' So I said, 'I mean, why can't you move on?' And she said, 'I am as far on as I intend to go without Sam.'"

"Who's Sam?"

"Her son?" Val took a sip of her tea.

"Her husband?" I conjectured.

"I thought we decided she was lesbian?" Val said.

"Well, that doesn't mean she wasn't married, for heaven's sake." I looked to Ford for support, but she was silent. "Really, you straight people can be so dense sometimes. Like being lesbian means being only one way."

"Well, we sure know there's more than one way to be a spirit. Your Camille is quite a character."

"Camille? You say her name is Camille?"

"Did I leave that out? She did identify herself."

"Camille what?"

"I don't know. I didn't think to ask."

"Well, I'm miffed, actually." I crossed my arms

and tapped one foot on the floor. "She sure never spoke to me, and I'm the one she ... she what?"

"Loves, I think. I think *you* are who she meant by 'us.' Like Mrs. B, I think Camille has the hots for you."

"So who the hell is Sam?"

Ford spoke at last. "Probably her goddamn dead dog. I've had enough of this. I gotta get out of here."

Val rose as Ford stalked out of the room, out of the house.

"Well, I guess she believes me now," I said.

Val put her arms around me. "Look kiddo, this has been a pretty stressful evening. We all need time to sort through it all, Ford included. I'll talk to her on the way home, okay?"

I nodded and she continued to hold me as if we'd been friends since birth. "If you need anything, ever, you let me know, okay?"

She put her hands on my shoulders. "Mel, be careful, okay? Please be careful."

"Sure, but ... what about Camille? *I* want to talk to her."

"I have a strong feeling she'll find a way to communicate with you. You could try the automatic writing. I don't think she'll just give up. I think she'll try again. I only wish I could be here. Good night, Mel. I loved, absolutely loved meeting you."

She looked around the room and said to the air, "And you, too."

Chapter 12

Ford's reaction worried me. I needed to talk to her, reassure her, calm her. The next day I went to the corner bar to make the call. The same cute bartender was working, busy with customers, but she smiled and waved at me.

First I called the golf course but they told me she'd called in sick.

"Sick?" I said to the woman receptionist. "She never gets sick."

"Hey," she answered, "the boss calls in sick — she's sick."

"Look, would you please tell her Mel called? It's important."

Then I called her apartment. Her line was busy. I redialed, thinking I'd misdialed the first time. Ford has call waiting. I tease her that her call waiting has call waiting. She can't bear to miss a call.

Well, I comforted myself, she can't be too sick if she can sit and yak on the phone. Maybe she was on long distance. I dialed one more time. Still busy. She could be carrying on two conversations at once, I thought. I've seen her do it.

A woman, I figured. Women. Smiling at my assumed solution, I turned to leave. Halfway out the door I heard a guy at the bar call out, "Another round here, Bonnie m'love."

Bonnie. So her name was Bonnie. I'd remember that. To make sure, I repeated it all the way home, adding the "m'love" as if it were her last name.

As I stepped in the door, I noticed again how beautiful the rugs looked on the newly finished floors. There were a few worn spots, a few places where the hand-knotted fringe was missing, but this didn't diminish their appeal.

I walked from room to room, pleased with the effect. At the doorway to the green room I stood for a moment. The philodendron was recovering quickly. It occurred to me that it might do better still if I raised it off the floor so it could get more sun. It might even like some company. If I were a house plant I wouldn't want to be the only one, I thought. I knew little about plants but decided to learn, decided to get "Phyl," as I'd started to call her, some company.

And I would build something to raise them up to at least windowsill level. I would make the green room as green as I could. The coffee table I'd thrown together worked, so I thought to make another just like it for the plants I planned to get. I went to the lower level of the barn and sorted through the crates again, stacking the best two outside in the sun.

The barnwood was on the main floor and I went there to see what plank might fit without sawing. The bookshelf planks had been like cutting through iron.

There was one that I judged might do, and then I glanced up at the loft. There were all kinds of odd bits of lumber up there. Maybe I could find something in the loft that would be easier to work with. Maybe I could even make a multiple-tiered plant stand.

The ladder to the loft looked rickety and, as I'd noticed the first day, a third of its rungs were gone. I'm scared shitless on ladders. I don't remember ever falling, or even seeing anyone fall. But I don't trust them. At all.

I hadn't wanted to explore the loft before, but now I was on a mission. Maybe up there I would find some nice pine pieces. They wouldn't have to be more than three feet long or even free of knots or warps.

The missing rungs were spaced so that access was possible and I climbed carefully. The old splintery wood protested but held.

It was dark up there. The light socket was installed under the loft. I kept away from the huge wasp nest in the highest peak and balanced each step through the stacked discards. Old window frames, old doors, countless bits and pieces of wood and wire, rope and even half a garden hose had been tossed up there for storage instead of being tossed out, which is what I thought most of it should have been. There was broken glass too; some of the window frames hadn't been empty when first put up there.

Through the darkness I peered for some glimmer of light wood. I had my heart set on a pine plank or two and was so focused it felt as if I could almost will it into existence. I was so concentrated on finding something light I almost missed what was shoved back into the a dark corner. The floor beneath me gave a few times. The loft wasn't made for this, I realized, not for supporting a moving human weight.

Deep in the darkness, against the slope of the roof was a darker rectangle. A box of some kind, I thought, or maybe a trunk.

The wood scraps made getting to the box difficult and the floor gave again as I tried. It was easy to imagine my body falling through and lying in a grotesque heap, covered with a small mountain of wood scraps and trash, my head twisted unnaturally. Who would find me? And how long would it take?

I shook myself out of this macabre vision and shifted my weight again. The floor held. On my hands and knees, I crawled to the box which had metal clasps, a lock. It was a trunk, wide and low and coated with dust and mouse turds. The metal parts were rusted but not so much that I couldn't unlatch the clasps and raise the unlocked lid an inch or two. But the angle of the barn's roof prevented my opening it completely. It was, I realized with delight, just the right size for the spot under the window in the green room. It was the perfect plant stand. All I'd have to do was scrub it down, maybe let it sun for a day. But how to get it down? How to get it down from the loft?

Reaching around to its sides, I found the leather strap handles I expected to. One of them, I could feel, was broken, but the other felt solid. I reclasped the lid and went to retrieve the length of rope I'd seen. It was unfrayed, but I wasn't sure it was long enough. It was all I had; it would have to do. I pulled the trunk away from the dark corner, tied the rope to the leather handle, and shoved the trunk to the edge of the loft. I hoped the strap would hold, the rope too. I didn't think about anything breakable being in the trunk, but I didn't want to dent it up either. Slowly I eased the trunk over the edge and toward the barn floor. The sisal rope burned my hands and I had to use my shirt as makeshift gloves. I regretted not bringing some with me in the first place. Although the trunk was not terribly heavy, my raw hands and the creaking of the loft's floor added to my anxiety. Finally I heard a faint thunk and felt the rope slacken, then climbed down the ladder.

In the light I could see it wasn't really black, but dark green and made of a sturdy but somewhat flexible material I could not identify. As I dragged it fully into the sun that streamed through the barn door, I made a mental note to research trunk constructions of the past.

Although awkward, it wasn't heavy so I knew it wasn't full of gold or priceless contraband. But as I knelt before the trunk I was suddenly filled with an overpowering sense of dread. I ached to leave the trunk alone, closed and alone in the barn. *Put it back. Put it back. Forget you ever saw it,* I told myself. My hands shook as I lifted the lid. The divided set-in compartment was empty — nothing more than dust and flakes of the trunk's paper lining. The trunk itself, I sensed, had not cost anyone very much money. The tray, fragile and flimsy, I set aside to examine the few contents nestled underneath. A bulky bundle, wrapped carefully in many layers of flannel, held an old oil lamp, empty of oil, its chimney intact thanks to the careful wrapping. Plain, utilitarian and cheap, it was also, I was sure, still functional. Great, I thought, wondering if lamp oil gave off fumes as bad as kerosene. Another thing to research. Maybe I could sniff some at the hardware store. Kerosene fumes knock me on my ass.

Next I found a black wool man's suit, quaint but smelling too heavily of must and dust to tolerate. I took them outside to air as I finished unpacking.

Between the suit of clothes and another flannel-wrapped package was a composition notebook, the cardboard cover printed black and white to look marbleized. Again my hands shook. Was this a journal? A diary? Were there sweet or terrible secrets in its pages? Hope and trepidation warred within me. Hope won and I opened the cover. But again I was disappointed, and relieved too. It was nothing but the lessons of someone trying to teach a child to write. Two different handwritings, one neat and sure, printing the letters of the alphabet one to a page, upper case then lower case. Then an unsteady hand had poorly imitated the first over and over. The pages went on and on, painstaking effort and frustrating attempts. Toward the end the student began to show progress, had linked letters to form simple words. The first word was a name: *SAM*. So he had learned that much at least. I was glad for him, but the child's primer gave no clue to his identity or relationship to Camille. Her son? Possibly a brother? I put the notebook aside, realizing I might never know any more than I did at that moment.

One large bundle remained, wrapped like the lamp in flannel, and like the clothes, intolerable to my nose, so I took it outside. Although it had been folded with the topside in, I knew it was a quilt by the tiny neat stitches on the muslin backing. Eagerly but carefully, I opened it to the sun. It was old, the fabric stiffer and coarser than our cottons today, but it looked like new, as if it had never been used. Bright colors leaped free as I opened the quilt all the way out and draped it across the tall grass. The simple pattern of blocks and triangles was arranged into squares which repeated between borders. But the colors were vibrant and surprising — red and purple with only small amounts of white as background.

"Red and purple," I said aloud, "I wouldn't use those colors together." Then I laughed at myself for being so narrow. The quilt was beautiful and the sun was shining and I was young and alive. Why not put red and purple together? Why not put red and purple with green? It belonged in the green room, I thought.

"Thank you," I said, again to no one.

Forgetting the trunk, I gathered up the quilt and carried it at arm's length to the house. I set the washer on delicate, warm-cold, and added a minimum of liquid detergent. When the cycle was complete, I took the clean, wet quilt down the hill to the clothesline. A ripple of pleasure went through me as I did this simple task. There was nothing in the world except for me and the quilt and the bright October sun. I sat on one of the crates and thought what a fool I'd been to be afraid earlier. How wise it was for me to ignore that primitive fear. Look what came of overcoming unfounded terror, of facing my silly fear. I had a new plant stand and a new oil lamp and a gorgeous new quilt. As I watched the wind gently ruffle its edges, I thought what a beautiful thing the quilt was, there on the line in the sun.

Eventually I remembered the clothes, the trousers and jacket cut in a narrow, uncomfortable-looking style. I went for them and hung them to air on the line: the suit, the white shirt, the suspenders. Could these be washed? I didn't want to risk it, but airing them would help. Braces, I thought. That's what they used to call suspenders.

Thoroughly pleased with myself and my finds, I went back into the barn for the lamp and the trunk, planning to scrub them down and air the trunk. As

I tipped the trunk to drag it up the hill, I heard a clunk. I'd missed something. Lowering the trunk, I looked inside, reached in and drew out a gun. It was old, crude and simple, but most assuredly a gun.

Chapter 13

Mrs. B needed thanking. I sat at Rosa, composing a note to her — short, grateful, mildly flirtatious.

It felt good. It wasn't really writing, but it felt good. Although I still attended classes occasionally, I wasn't doing any of the work and I certainly wasn't working on my writing. I printed out the thank you note and began a generic catch-up letter to friends I hadn't contacted since graduation. A little like cheating, I'd change the salutations and the last line, then send the same letter to everyone, I thought. Even if they caught on, they'd forgive me.

Carrying the master copy up to my room to revise, I left Rosa on again, thinking I'd be right back. Instead I fell asleep. Hours later I awoke, brought out of another wandering dream by the familiar clack of Rosa's keys. Not fast, but clear. Clack. Clack. Clack.

In just my Adrian nightshirt, heart pounding, I cautiously went to investigate, hesitating at the top of the stairs. What if there was a prowler, a rapist, a thief? Right. Typing, I thought, I'm sure that happens a lot. A marauding typist, a walkaway from some typing-pool prison. It was probably some kind of short in Rosa's circuitry.

Summoning a courage I did not feel, I went slowly down the stairs to the empty rooms, silent except for the occasional clacking. And then it stopped.

With disbelief I stared at Rosa's screen. Val had not prepared me for this.

I fed her a fresh sheet of thermal transfer paper and pressed the print key. With one short hum the words appeared: *besamforme.*

No spaces, no caps, but the message seemed clear, if not the meaning. At least not at first.

My initial reaction was to tear the paper out, wad it up, toss it away, switch Rosa off and go back to bed — deny, in effect, that this had ever happened. But I knew that turning off Rosa was one thing, turning off my mind was another. There was no way I could sleep after this.

The other alternative was to explore it, experience it, allow it. Even encourage it. Whatever it was, wherever it would take me. The second choice, the one that made me shiver, was the most tempting.

"Okay," I said to the empty room, "I'm in."

The decision to type my questions instead of simply speak them aloud stemmed from the place in me that constantly takes notes. This way I would have hard copy of both sides of the conversation, which I realized bleakly would prove absolutely nothing to a skeptic. But any answers I got would be priceless to me.

I said "First there are some things you need to know that will help me. This is the space bar, use it between words." I demonstrated. "This is called a shift key. When you press it at the same time you press a letter it makes that letter a capital. I guess we can skip the touch typing lessons for now."

Then, not sure what would happen or if anything would, I typed.

What is your name? It seemed a logical place to start.

For a brief moment, nothing happened and my hopes sank. But then the answer came, slowly, haltingly, one letter at a time: *camille carr.*

So that is your name, I thought. Val was right about that too. Then, before I could print out, more words appeared: *what is yours.*

"Wait a minute," I said, printing what she'd written and then switching Rosa to her higher memory capacity. I'd print it all out later, I decided, so we wouldn't be interrupted. Then I answered: *Melanie Myer.*

Camille wrote: *i like you melanie how old are you.*

I answered: *I'm 23.*

C: *me too funny coincidence.*

Then I felt awkward. I didn't want to offend her, to lose this contact, and I didn't know how to broach the sensitive topic I needed to. I tried to be diplomatic.

M: *Camille, are you alive?*

C: *not like you are not any more.*

M: *Since when? I mean, when did you stop being alive like me?*

C: *on saturday june 6 1914.*

M: *What happened?*

C: *something went wrong between sam and me.*

M: *Who is Sam?*

C: *my love.*

M: *What went wrong?*

C: *dont know we were supposed to go together.*

M: *Go where?*

C: *here.*

M: *You mean die?*

C: *die together me first then sam.*

M: *What happened?*

C: *dont know lost sam.*

M: *Sam died?*

C: *no me sam to join me did not did not lost sam.*

A wave of aching loss overwhelmed me; the room throbbed with it. The air and my heart were filled with a terrible anguish, a devastating sense of loss. I fought the urge to cry, fought to keep control of my emotions and this connection.

M: *Camille, I want to keep talking to you. Stay with me.*

C: *you remind me of sam.*

M: *I do? In what way? Looks?*

I was grateful for this topic switch.

C: *a little sam is taller same eyes hair color something else demeanor hard worker.*

M: *Sam was a hard worker?*

C: *yes sam worked for me we fell in love.*

M: *What kind of work did Sam do?*

C: *farming my parents died in a train wreck and left me the farm i could not work the farm alone sam came looking for work at just the right time so handsome so strong and a hard worker sam lived here.*

M: *Here? You mean in this house?*

C: *yes it was the foremans cabin before there were other workers too but no crew after no money to pay them.*

M: *And you and he fell in love.*

C: *no silly not he she sam is a woman.*

So Val was right about this, too. I had a lesbian ghost. I smiled and continued.

M: *You hired a woman farmhand? Was that common?*

C: *no i hired a man never heard of a woman farmhand.*

M: *So you didn't know she was a woman?*

C: *no not for a long time show me again capitals.*

That threw me for a second, but then I got it and demonstrated the shift and punctuation keys.

C: *I was surprised.*

M: *How did you find out?*

C: *I came here to bring her a present a quilt I made you have it bears claw quilt I was going to spread it on her bed as a surprise I was already in love I already wanted Sam I found her rags drying.*

M: *Rags?*

C: *monthly rags.*

M: *Were you angry? Confused?*

C: *I was relieved never wanted a man I do not like men.*

M: *Me neither, not much.*

C: *I know you are like us like me like Sam.*

M: *Yes, I'm a dyke.*

C: *dyke I do not know that word.*

M: *Lesbian with an attitude.*

C: *we never used a word we just were but I like dyke I like your big dyke friend too.*

M: *Ford?*

C: *yes Ford she is funny she tells funny stories has a nice laugh attractive.*

M: *You are attracted to Ford?*

C: *yes and you.*

M: *Me? You are attracted to me?*

C: *very much you are so much like Sam.*

M: *Do you mean because I work hard and wear pants?*

C: *yes mens clothes you are so masculine.*

Then I got it. And blushed. And changed the subject.

M: *Tell me about Sam. Where did Sam come from?*

C: *She never told me. Jackson, I thought.*

M: *Did she have family?*

C: *She told me her mother died. She had six younger sisters. Her father made her work like a man on the farm. That's how she learned to do the work I hired her to do. She told me he started wanting her to do other things, too, that she did not want to do. So one night she took his best clothes, cut off her hair, and left. She took his gun, too.*

M: *What about her sisters? She left them with him?*

C: *What could she do? Do not judge her. She could not stay there.*

M: *I don't mean to be judgmental. I'm sorry. I just don't think I could have left my sisters behind.*

C: *Do you have sisters?*

M: *No. I'm an only child.*

C: *Then how do you know what you would do?*

M: *I'm sorry. You're right. Let's keep talking.*

C: *Is this talking?*

M: *It'll have to do for now. But tell me more about you and Sam.*

C: *Sam carved my name in a ceiling beam.*

M: *How romantic. Like instead of a tree?*

C: *She teased me about carving my name in the willow tree I planted for her.*

M: *A willow tree? There is a huge willow in the side yard. It was how I found this house in the first place. Do you mean that one?*

C: *Huge? There is only the little one I put in. It is really just a branch of the one near my house, but I knew it would take root and grow. It was too small to carve on. I would not let her. But she was only teasing.*

M: *Camille, it's been over eighty years since you planted it.*

C: *Eighty?*

M: *Yes.*

C: *Eighty years.*

Then the keys fell silent for several minutes. Finally they clacked again.

C: *Then it is a good thing that I died when I did. I would be very old by now.*

M: *When were you born?*

C: *March 2, 1891.*

M: *How old was Sam?*

C: *Fifteen months older than me. I teased her about being such an old man.*

M: *Where were you born?*

C: *Savannah, Georgia. My mother named me for the flowers she loved. They will not grow here. My grandfather painted her a picture of white camellias. He was an artist. The picture hung in our house. That was how I found out Sam could not read.*

M: *Sam couldn't read? She had a lot of secrets, didn't she?*

C: *Do not make fun of Sam.*

M: *I'm sorry. I didn't mean it like that. Please keep talking. Tell me this story.*

C: *This is not a story this is true.*

M: *I didn't mean it like that. Tell me about finding out that Sam could not read. Please.*

But it took her a minute, long enough for me to worry that I'd ruined everything. The chill in the air expressed her irritation, then finally she typed again.

C: *I know you are not mean. I love Sam.*

M: *I know. And I'm sure she loved you.*

C: *Yes she does. She saw the painting in my house and I told her what it meant and about how I got my name. She remembered the picture when she bought me a birthday present. A bottle of gardenia perfume with the label like the ones in the picture. She thought it was a bottle of camellia perfume. I laughed at her and hurt her feelings. She did not know the difference and she did not know camellias have no perfume. I did not know she could not read. So I started to teach her. Only she was still he to me then. I had not discovered her secret yet. Our first kiss was as man and woman. My first kiss from a man. I thought that was why I had never wanted a man before because I was waiting for Sam. When I found out I laughed. Sam did not. Sam was ashamed. She was tormented.*

M: *Because she couldn't read?*

C: *No because she was not a man. She said she was not a woman either. She said she was nothing.*

M: *But you didn't feel ashamed? I mean, to be a woman in love with another woman?*

C: *No. She said we were wrong. Something was wrong with us. I felt whole, happy to be with her and —*

The keyboard fell silent. I realized we'd been at this for three hours. The mood in the air changed again, shifted subtly. Her mood became mine.

M: *And what, Camille?*

C: *— on fire. I burned for Sam, for her kisses, for her caresses, for her touch. I longed for more much much much more.*

I blushed, shared her fever. I could try to ignore the implications of her words, but I could not ignore my own responses to her words and to her energy. I could not deny the tightening of my vagina, the heat building there, the dampness I suddenly felt, the tightness and heightened sensitivity of my nipples brushing the fabric of my cotton nightshirt. I struggled to maintain control of my response and of the conversation.

M: *You said Sam didn't laugh much. What did make her laugh?*

C: *Me. I could make her laugh. We laughed finally about the gardenia perfume. She would call me her little gardenia and I called her my big passion flower. I wore her gardenia perfume every day so we could always have the things we could not have here. Gardenias, camellias, and love.*

M: *Did you make love?*

C: *We kissed and hugged and flirted. I could not keep my hands off her.*

M: *No. I mean did you consummate your love? Did you sleep together? Did you have sex?*

The urge to touch myself was too strong; it overpowered me. I began to brush my hands across my nipples as I waited for her answer. My right hand moved down and between my legs. I was amazed at how wet I was, at the urgency of my need to be touched, to touch. I had been dry, unarousable since Becca. I probed and stroked, moaning, sobbing for release which came suddenly, startlingly as I circled my clit. I cried out one loud and lonely wordless cry, then bent forward in my chair, hugging myself and allowing tears of pleasure, of release. The keys clicked again.

C: *I did that too. Sometimes Sam would watch me but she would not touch me that way and would not let me touch her. She said it was a sin. It was wrong. Do you think it is wrong?*

M: *No. Absolutely not. I think sex is human and exciting and wonderful. I think it heals. Hearts and souls and bodies, if it is done with love.*

C: *Do you have someone to touch that way? Do you have someone to touch you?*

M: *No. Not now. I had a girlfriend but we broke up. There is no one.*

C: *Do you want someone?*

And I didn't answer, couldn't answer. I felt as if I were slipping, sliding down some kind of ravine, faster and faster with less and less control. Or desire for it.

The keys clattered.

Melanie. Melanie. Please. Be Sam for me.

Chapter 14

On Wednesdays I could count on getting the local weekly newspaper. At first I thought it was a mistake, having neither ordered nor paid for a subscription. The last tenants, I figured, had forgotten to change their address. But one day when I encountered my neighbor collecting her own mail, she explained that it came free and always had.

"Except," she said, "that might change. Now that the kids are running things, there's talk they may start to charge. I don't know what we'll do then. Get it, I suppose, it'd seem strange without it. Still . . ."

Then she wandered up to her house still talking but no longer to me.

None of what she said interested me, nor did most of the local news items like — promotions at such and such a bank, graduations or engagements, weddings. Every once in a while some local kid would be named to the dean's list at Saginaw Valley, my old school, and that would catch my eye. The seemingly endless and often comical infighting among the area's village, township or police boards tended to be reported with an enthusiasm past duty. Sometimes, there'd be a recipe I'd tear out and forget to try.

There was a weekly column I enjoyed. Rae Wheeler wrote about home and car repair and maintenance for the totally unskilled and terrified to try. She wrote frequently about her old green pickup truck, anthropomorphizing it in the same way I did with Subie and Rosa. I liked her sardonic humor and unfailing determination to try, to learn, to conquer. She was, I strongly suspected, a screaming, stomping dyke. After one specific column, I knew for sure. She apparently fixed a bookshelf that had caved in but then, after the repair was complete, she got sidetracked by thinking about rereading her favorites. Among others, she listed Rita Mae Brown, Marge Piercy, Lisa Alther, Georgia Cottrell and Carol Schmidt. Occasionally, I'd fantasize about going to the newspaper office to meet her, on the pretext of having lost my copy of *Silverlake Heat* and asking to borrow hers. I imagined us becoming friends. But that seemed too pushy so I never did.

I also read the personal column in the want ads. While there was seldom much intriguing, I did chuckle over the woman who was looking for someone with a pontoon boat to give her a ride on one of the area's many lakes, and the one who was looking to trade fresh brown eggs for a piano.

It was easy to tell when the paper ran out of local news because they would fill with house plans or canned historical perspectives.

So I pulled the paper out of the mailbox on this particular Wednesday and started up the embankment. It came folded in half crosswise, front page up. Bold black block print proclaimed *The Courier* and directly beneath that were words I'd overlooked many times. On this day they jumped out at me: *Since 1887*. And I thought: Gee, since before Camille was even born, that's pretty amazing. And then I took a few more steps and thought: Gee, maybe they have an old copy with her birth announcement in it. But no, that wasn't right, she wasn't born here.

And then I stopped completely, stunned by my next thought. Maybe they had an old copy with the account of her death.

Her death. The paper must have a morgue, no, call it a library. I could look it up. I could verify her birth, her death, her existence. At the very least, I thought, they'd have old copies, maybe even on microfilm.

I decided not to tell Camille, to surprise her. I wondered how I'd like to read my own obituary. Well, I reasoned, trying to be rational, if I were a ghost already, it might be okay.

The next day I drove the seven miles to Michigan's Brooklyn, to the newspaper office, a long, narrow one-story cement-block building with a light brick facade. There was no old green truck in the parking lot so I abandoned my hope of meeting my columnist.

"I'd like to look through your back issues," I told the receptionist, not knowing how much of my purpose she would need or want to know, or how much I'd want to tell her.

"For this month?" she asked, with an expression of disbelief, as if I'd asked to look through her underwear drawer.

"Well, no. Actually for 1914."

"What?"

I repeated my request and she answered, "Well, I don't know. You wait here. I'll get it for you. We can't let just anyone back there you know."

She sniffed in totally unreasonable disapproval and bustled through a door.

"So who fucking asked you to," was my imaginary response to her rudeness. Then I busied myself visualizing her twisting an ankle on her silly teetery high heels, or her reaction when they discover blue eyeshadow causes cancer. She'll really be in for it then, I thought, smiling with petty vindictive pleasure.

She caught me smiling as she returned carrying what looked like a huge storybook. She must've thought I was smiling at her, not about her eminent demise or disfigurement, because her tone softened.

"I'm afraid these are pretty dusty," she said. "We started the new binding in 'thirty-five so these older ones are pretty brittle. Let me know if I can help you," she offered, returning to her desk and the ringing telephone.

"*Courier,*" she said briskly into the phone, seeming to forget me entirely.

The only places for me to open up the huge volume were either on the floor or on a shelf of wedding invitation and business stationery sample books.

I chose the shelf, precariously balancing the book on top of sample personalized cocktail napkins and souvenir wedding matchbooks. Maybe I'd come here, I mused, if I ever got married. Would they print napkins with two veils or two top hats? What would Miss Priss think when I told her we wanted "Melanie and Rae" on the matches. Or, on the invitations: "Melanie and Mary, commitment-minded and politically-correct dykes, having no other models than traditional Judeo-Christian, heterosexual, patriarchal customs rooted in concepts of ownership and protection of patrilinear bloodlines, cordially invite you . . ."

I figured Miss Priss would refuse the order but it would be fun to try. Maybe I'd place the order, just to push her buttons. That might be amusing.

I was stalling and I knew it. The hard-bound back issues lay before me. I knew the date of her death. It wasn't as if I were about to discover that Camille was dead. Of course she was dead, that's how she got to be a ghost. Still, I inexplicably resisted doing the very thing I had gone there to do.

Immediately upon opening the book, I regretted not bringing my dust mask. Gingerly I turned the brittle sepia pages, regretting their disturbance. An intruder, that's what I felt like, a snoop, an uninvited and unwanted guest. Dust rose and ticked my nose. My hands immediately felt dirty and I longed to wash them.

A few headlines caught my eye. Except for clothing and hairstyle fashions in the photographs, much seemed familiar: local politics criticized; local patrons fawned over; local youngsters promoted.

Then, there it was, on the front page of June 10:

Young Cement City
Woman Found Dead

"The body of Miss Camille Carr of Cement City" it read, "was discovered Saturday, reports police chief William Rogers. Suicide is the suspected cause of death, given the location and condition of the body. Although little is known at this juncture, investigators speculate that Miss Carr was despondent over a personal matter. Police seek to question a former employee of Miss Carr's, Mr. Samuel Morehouse, but his whereabouts are unknown. The discovery of Miss Carr's body was made by her cousin, Miss Samantha Carr of Chicago, who thereupon notified police. Although distraught at the loss of her cousin, Miss S. Carr informed police that her cousin was deeply enamored of Mr. Morehouse and was inconsolable at his departure shortly previous to the tragedy. Chief Rogers speculates that Miss C. Carr's suicide stemmed from this unrequited affection. Temporarily, Miss Samantha Carr will continue her stay at her deceased cousin's home. An obituary, detailing funeral arrangements, may be found on page seven."

* * * * *

I turned to page seven. The item was brief.

"Miss Camille Carr, born in Savannah, Georgia in 1891, died June 6 of self-inflicted gunshot wounds. Preceding her in death are her parents, Mr. and Mrs. Simon Carr, also formerly of Georgia. The Carr family moved to Cement City in 1903. Surviving her is one cousin, Miss Samantha Carr of Chicago. The funeral for Miss Carr will be Tuesday, June 11 at two o'clock in the afternoon at Gugel's Funeral Home in Cement City. Interment will be at Brookside Cemetery."

And that was it. I turned back to the news story and sat staring as tears gathered in my eyes. Well, what had I expected? A resurrection?

"Can I get a photocopy of this story?" I asked the receptionist. A copy machine stood behind her.

"Well," she said with her original peevish tone, "I can try but they usually don't come out too well when they're this old."

To her credit, she did try, but the cumbersome volume wasn't too cooperative. I didn't get the obituary, just the news item, and the background was almost as dark as the print. But I could read it.

I paid my dime and refrained from mentioning that she had, in fact, made two copies. Snoopy old thing, I thought, go ahead and read what I came here for. I didn't thank her and she didn't thank me, didn't even look at me with my probably red-rimmed eyes, either.

From M-50, I took the back road, Brooklyn

Highway, almost to US-12, inventing trivial destinies for what I estimated was a trivial woman. I pulled over onto the shoulder, fumbling for the barely decipherable copy stuffed into my back pocket.

There it was, in black and gray: "Discovery of the body was made by her cousin Samantha Carr..."

Her cousin Samantha? Samantha? Sam? Holy shit. Camille's Sam?

No. No way. That couldn't be.

Once home, I ran into the house, clutching the paper and calling Camille's name. I switched on Rosa and typed in my question for Camille: *Why didn't you tell me about your cousin from Chicago.*

After a minute or so, which seemed like weeks, her response clattered in. *I have no cousin.*

Chapter 15

Excited about the new twist in Camille's story, I called Ford at work from the corner bar. I couldn't wait to tell her, to tell someone else, what I'd found.

Ford had on her business voice when she answered, so I knew she was swamped. When business is slow her phone voice is seductive, flirtatious. She took the bar number and said she'd call me back.

"Might be a while," was her curt warning.

"I'll be here," I replied, understanding her

priorities but disappointed, too, and still eager to talk.

Bonnie was behind the bar. I'd grinned at her when I came in. Bonnie was a dyke. I just knew it.

The bar was nearly empty except for an arguing straight couple at a table against the far wall and a middle-aged man dressed in a worn-looking Western get-up. He played pool against himself, switching cues and keeping up a steady mutter of commentary.

Sliding up onto the stool nearest the pay phone, I glanced up to find Bonnie waiting expectantly, her hands resting on the bar's sunken edge, her arms wide apart. Her grin matched my own, the one I was still wearing, the one that was beginning to make my face ache with its unaccustomed presence.

From her contagious grin with its one misaligned front tooth, my gaze went to her eyes. With a mild start I realized they were slightly different colors, one bluish green, one yellowish green. The effect was startling and extremely attractive. As I wondered whether her eyes were that way naturally or if it was done with contacts, either deliberately or by accident, she blinked slowly and chuckled.

"It's natural. I was born this way. There's a lot of queer things about me," she said, never losing her grin.

Before I could recover from my initial surprise of her open use of the Q word, she spoke again. "Look, if we're going to do this all night long, we should maybe introduce ourselves?" She offered a hand across the bar. Her skin was warm, firm, solid, rough. We were still grinning like fools and I could not unlock my gaze from hers. "I'm Bonnie," she said.

"I know," I answered, reluctantly withdrawing my hand from hers.

"You know?"

"I've heard people call you that, when I've been in before."

"A few times, to use the phone. Quick in and quick out."

"I live up the road —"

"I know. The little gray house, right? With the willow tree?"

"How'd you know that?"

"Well, I know you drive that little gray Subaru with the duct tape. I've seen it parked up there on my way to and from work. I go right by there every day. I look for you."

"You look for me?"

"Yeah. I've tried to think of an excuse to stop over. I've wanted to meet you."

My grin dissolved over her last few remarks and I pulled back.

"Why?" I asked. "What do you want?"

Her gaze flicked across my face, her grin subsided to a smile. "Don't do that," she said. "Don't shut off. I just wanted to meet you, wanted to get to know you."

"Why?"

"Why? Why not? You interest me. I knew when I first saw you that we have some things in common. I'm curious about you — gray car, gray house, gray eyes, but not a gray person. Definitely not a gray person. Definitely not. You are ... fuchsia. Warm, exciting, exotic somehow. Tempting."

"Me? Tempting?" I laughed self-conscious at her words.

"Okay. You're not ready to hear that. Okay. How about cute? I think you're real cute." She grinned again, reached over and quickly squeezed my hand. "Now, how about a drink? What can I bring you?"

"Soda? With lime?"

"Out of limes."

"Lemon?"

"Lemons are way past their prime. How about orange? A fresh orange slice?"

I nodded and Bonnie set the glass in front of me, placing a cocktail napkin beneath it.

"How much?" I asked, reaching for my pocketful of change.

Bonnie shook her head. "That's on me. There's just one hitch. You have to tell me your name."

"Mel. Melanie. Lani. Not Melly. Never, ever Melly."

"I know. I'm lots of people too, depending on who's talking to me. My parents named me Bonita, but I'm Bonnie to myself. Some friends call me Bonn. Even Bon-Bon, but I don't allow that very much. Makes me sound edible. 'Course," she added, rolling her eyes and shrugging, "some say I am."

I blushed furiously as Bonnie glanced out at her few other customers. She drew two bottles of Budweiser and a can of Busch out of the coolers and came out from behind the bar. I took the opportunity to check her out more thoroughly. She wore black jeans, black low-heeled Western boots, a collarless white shirt with its long sleeves folded halfway up her forearms. No watch, no rings, but around her neck was a little lavender suede amulet pouch hung from a purple suede thong. Her hair

118

was short, dark with a lot of curls and waves that didn't look like she had tried too hard to tame them.

She took the Buds to the couple whose argument had apparently aroused them mightily. They were falling all over each other. The woman had moved her chair next to the man's and they were playing pretzel with their legs. Bonnie said something which made them both laugh. Then the man started petting the woman's hair as if she were an Irish Setter. And there was a resemblance — she was all puppyish and trying to please. He said something that made the woman lay her head against his beefy shoulder, which enhanced her setter image. Bonnie shook her head and chuckled, then collected their empties and their money.

She took the Busch to the pool player who had two dollars tucked under his empty. Without a word, she replaced the can and bills with the fresh beer and placed his change on the edge of the pool table. He continued his imaginary tournament as Bonnie returned to the bar and to me.

I said, "They didn't call for those. How did you know they were ready?"

"Oh, that's easy. I've got them on a timer." She laughed, ringing up the sale.

"What's in the bag?" I asked, gesturing to her amulet bag.

"Oh, right. It's a crystal," she said, working it partway out of its bag and leaning over the bar to show me.

I reached impulsively for it but she pulled away. "Don't," she said. "No one else is supposed to touch it." She tucked the flat clear stone back into the pouch and shook her head. "I don't know if that's true. I don't know how much I believe in it myself, except I feel compelled to wear it. Just a habit maybe. A friend gave it to me. It's supposed to enhance my psychic ability, my ESP."

"You're psychic?" I asked, suddenly interested in her on yet another level.

"Well, I believe we all are, to some degree. Other senses we take for granted unless we lose one. Or maybe one is extra sensitive. You know, like people who can read street signs from two blocks away or can smell something others can't. ESP isn't any more weird or special than sight or hearing or touch or taste. When we call it intuition, no one has any doubts. Call it psychic ability and people get twitchy. It's the same thing, just a different name. If I say 'olfactory ability,' people say 'What?' But if I say 'smell,' well, everyone knows exactly what I mean and there's no question that they can do it, right?"

"Right," I said, scrutinizing her. Could I talk to her about Camille? Would she understand?

"Oh, geez Louise, I've been soapboxing again. Sorry." She refilled my soda.

"No, don't be," I said, "I'm interested. Really. So you . . . you're sensitive? More, than most people?"

"Yeah, yeah, I guess I am. The friend who gave me the crystal thinks so."

"So, this friend who gave it to you, where is she now? It is a she?"

Bonnie nodded vigorously. "Yes, absolutely she. And she's in Colorado, trying to raise consciousnesses there."

"And this . . . sense you have . . ."

"We all have."

"Okay, but in you. Is it how you know what I'm going to say next, like about your eyes?"

"Well, everybody comments on my eyes."

"Then, how you knew when they were ready for another round?"

"Well, that's more like something you get a feel for when you've been doing it a while, but maybe, in a way, it does help. I think working with people sharpens those senses and, conversely, people with those senses are drawn to jobs working with people."

She paused for a second, examining my face closely before continuing. "Unless . . . unless they are afraid of that kind of perception. Then they might try to hide from it in solitary kinds of work. They might cut themselves off from others. Like you."

"Me?" I was surprised that the conversation so abruptly returned to me, and I was ready to protest.

"Don't bother to deny it. I'm not accusing you of anything. I'm just saying . . . you don't have to be . . . so alone."

Noisily, the couple got up to leave, gathering their things and helping each other to the door. " 'Night, Bonnie," they called, waving in our general direction.

Bonnie went out onto the floor and cleared their table, wiping it down and changing the ashtray. She brought back the empty bottles, dumping the dregs and clattering them into a beer case under the bar.

Glad for the diversion, I commented, "Glass bottles. I didn't even know beer still comes in glass bottles. Everything seems to be cans these days, or plastic."

"Well, as far as I'm concerned, that's one thing the boss does right. Even if it is a pain to deal with the empties sometimes."

"The boss? You don't own this place?"

"Nah, I just act like I do. My boss's name is Donna. Donna Kies. She and her realtor husband own the place but she won't let him anywhere near it. It's her baby, but she doesn't come in much herself except when they're fighting. Which is now, in fact. She should be here soon. He bought another new lawn tractor without asking her, so she's off again." Bonnie looked at me. "Yeah, I know, it sounds like she's a controlling bitch, but she's not really. She's a sweetheart. It's not about him not getting permission or anything. See, he's already got about eighteen lawn tractors. He just keeps buying them."

"Maybe he should open a dealership," I offered.

"Good idea. I'll suggest it. But really, you should see their house. They can't even use their garage and there are lawn tractors lined up outside, too, like golf carts."

At the word *golf*, I remembered Ford's promised call and the reason I needed to see her. Camille and Sam. For the first time, I realized I was not thinking solely about Camille. I was not thinking about the house, either, or planning improvements or repairs. I was relaxed and enjoying myself. But where did it go? How could I be so full of Camille for so long and then, in less than an hour, have all but forgotten her? Something like guilt crept in, or started to. Bonnie drove it off with her next words.

"Anyway, Donna will be here soon, so I'll get off

early. How about I come over for a while? We could continue our conversation, get better acquainted."

I hesitated, trying to decode "get better acquainted." Surely she didn't mean . . . After all, she was attractive as hell. I was almost shocked to discover my capability to respond. I was relieved, too. Becca hadn't destroyed me, despite everything. But to take someone I'd just met home with me? Was I ready for that? Did I even want to? On the other hand, if she meant "get acquainted" as in talk, exchange histories and backgrounds, likes and dislikes, goals and —

Bonnie reached across the bar again, squeezed my hand and brought me back to the Artesian Wells Bar, second stool from the end.

"Hey," she said. "I'm just talking about talking, here. I'm attracted and interested, but I don't dive until I know there's water in the pool, and no sharks. You know? Talk." I smiled my relief at her and she shook her head. "Did anyone ever tell you that you think too much?"

"Once or twice, when they weren't telling me I don't think at all."

"Then they don't know you."

Our eyes met and again I felt my tensions dissipate. For just that second, nothing mattered except her exquisite eyes, the strength of her hand and the calmness that emanated from her.

"So?" she asked. "Want company?"

Again I hesitated, for just a heartbeat.

"Unless there's a problem?" she said. "Are you with someone?"

Well, was I? How to answer? How to explain?

With theatrical timing, the pay phone behind me rang. Bonnie busied herself by wiping down the spotless bar, but I saw disappointment on her face nonetheless. As the phone rang a second time, it occurred to me that the beautiful, glib, self-possessed and charming Bonnie might be lonely, as isolated dealing with hundreds of people as I felt with nearly none.

I picked up the phone. "Ford?"

"What if it hadn't been me?" She sounded calmer. "Ford, you have to come out. Can you come out? I have to talk to you. I went to the newspaper office, looked up old papers. I think Sam cross-dressed again after Camille's death. I think she stuck around for a while, in Camille's house, posing as her cousin. But I can't figure out why. Wouldn't that be a weird thing to do? But see, they were looking to question the handyman. Get it? Not a woman, not a female cousin of Camille's. You have to come out. Please, please, please. I think we can figure this all out."

Ford's silence threw me off for a second. Then I remembered. She'd been swamped with work.

"You must be exhausted. I'm sorry. I know how busy you are. But think of it as R and R. Stay over, several days even. You can sit in the sun, soak up some quiet."

"I can't take off more than one day, Mel, really not even that. But I'll work the day shift tomorrow, come out and stay with you tomorrow night. We'll talk. We need to talk."

She did sound tired but I was sure our visit would revive her. I needed her. I needed to bounce my theories off her.

"Ford," I said, "I think Sam murdered Camille."

Ford was silent again. It was a horrible thought, I knew. Murder.

Finally she said, "I'll be out tomorrow. About six." Then her tone changed, lightened a little. "How about you make that vegetarian lasagna for me, Mel? With the spinach?"

"Anything for you baby, anything at all," I cooed in the pseudoseductive voice we used on each other. Her relaxed tone reassured me. If Ford was talking food, everything would be okay.

"Tomorrow," she promised.

After we hung up, I turned to look for Bonnie. She was talking with a fortyish woman with stiffly styled blonde hair piled in complicated curls. The woman twitched her head angrily from side to side, punctuating a lengthy complaint. Bonnie leaned toward her, whispering something as near to the woman's ear as she could get through the hair. The woman threw her head back and laughed. She gave Bonnie a backslap and moved behind the bar, trading places with her.

I waited by the door as Bonnie said goodbye to the woman I knew must be Donna, her boss.

"Good night," she said to me as she passed by and out the door.

I followed, catching her by the sleeve. "Wait," I said, "Bonnie?"

Her face was impassive, which confused me at first. Then I thought of how carefully I guarded my own emotions.

"Do you still want to come over?" I asked.

"Didn't you just get a better offer?"

"What?"

"The phone call."

"Ford? Good God, no. She's my best friend, my . . . pal, if that's not too queer a word."

Bonnie smiled then, which lit her whole face. Her eyes sparkled like two different kinds of jewels — tourmaline, maybe, and topaz.

"Well," she said. "I happen to like queer words. Love 'em, in fact. Are you sure? I mean, are you sure you want me? I mean to come? I mean to come over?"

We both laughed at her unintentional innuendos.

"Bonita," I said, with an exaggerated Latin accent, "I am very, very sure."

And I was. I was very, very sure as we got into our respective cars, as we crunched our way over the parking lot's new gravel and past the garishly painted concrete wall around the artesian spring which trickled pure clean water continuously. I was absolutely positive as she followed me past the old ornate farmhouse which owned not one speck of paint but a fleet of Mercedes and a free-roaming flock of chickens. I was sure as we passed my landlady's house. I was even sure as we slowed in front of my neighbors' green cinderblock house and waited for a semi to pass before turning into the driveway.

Then my certainty evaporated. Completely.

Bonnie tried to joke and make small talk as we stepped up into the porch. As we entered the kitchen she touched my arm, turning me to face her, but I couldn't look at her. I couldn't speak or respond at all. She took my face in her hands and made me meet her gaze. She looked into my eyes with a question in hers. Then she released me and walked slowly through the house. Her steps echoed clearly on the wood floors, were muffled when she walked across rugs. I heard her progress through each room, stopping once at the foot of the stairs, but not ascending. She paused again in the front bedroom. Ashamed, I leaned against the stove, feeling as if she'd just found out I was married. When she returned I fought for the strength to look at her.

"Geez Louise, it's true." She hugged herself for warmth. The house was cold, so very cold. "I'd heard rumors. When I was asking around, trying to find out more about you, no one knew anything about you, but everyone knew about the house. And it's true, isn't it? This house is haunted."

I said nothing. I could not have spoken if I'd wanted to. And I didn't want to.

"But it's more than that, isn't it?" she prodded. When I didn't answer, she reached out to me, her hands on my upper arms. "Mel?"

But I had no words, nothing to say.

She walked to the dining room door and stood there as if assessing the room's dimensions. Finally she turned, shaking her head as if to clear it.

"Mel, can we talk about this, about any of this? Maybe I can help."

I stared at the floor with my arms crossed in front of me. She waited, tried again, but I would not, could not, respond.

"Okay, look, maybe this was a mistake, but I don't think so. I think I can help, I want to. I didn't know exactly what it was, but I knew you were in some kind of trouble. I can't help if you won't talk to me, Mel. So I'm going to go home now. I guess

I'm not really wanted here, at least not yet. But you know where to find me. When you're ready, please, please contact me. Mel, are you listening? I don't know what's going on here, but I sure can see the effect it has on you. I don't know how to break through this . . . this prison you're in. But I'm sure willing to try. Just let me know, okay? Okay?"

I managed to nod, then Bonnie touched my arm and left. I didn't watch her leave but I heard her car door shut. It was several moments before her engine started and several more before I heard her pull away. As the hum of her car receded, the coldness did too. The house warmed and the sweet scent of gardenias filled the air. Rosa clattered for a few seconds and I went to read the message Camille wrote.

I don't like your friend.

Chapter 16

I was layering the lasagna when Ford pulled in.
She unloaded her truck as I poured water into the
corners of the glass pan, covered it with foil and put
it in the oven. She smiled and hugged me, but her
usual smartass remarks were missing.

"More tea?" I asked, automatically moving to
refill her ever-present water bottle. "I'm really glad
you could come, babe," I told her, hugging her
precious girth again. "And for overnight, even? What
a rare honor."

But my attempts to jolly her into our usual banter fell flat.

"Is something wrong?" I finally asked. "Woman trouble?"

Ford looked at me, silent at first; she seemed to be examining me, but for what?

"In a little bit," was her odd reply. "I need to feel right about this, need to say it just right. Give me a little more time, okay?"

"Oh, my God, you want a divorce. Ford, how could you do this to me? Is it another woman?"

But again, my joking didn't lighten her mood. Her dark eyes seemed sad, her face drawn. She kept watching me until I felt downright uncomfortable.

We made small talk until the lasagna was done. That is, I made small talk in the form of simple direct questions which she answered monosyllabically.

"How's work?"

" 'Kay."

"That new girl work out?"

"Yup."

"She a dyke?"

"Guess."

"She cute?"

"Yeah."

"You gonna move on her?"

"Nope."

"Think she'll move on you?"

"Nah."

"Heard from Carmen and Nancy?"

"Nope."

"Heard from Sandy?"

"Yup."

"How's she doing? Met anyone yet?"

Like that, on and on until I was ready to scream.

We cut huge squares of lasagna and headed for the couch to eat.

"I didn't make a salad," I said, explaining instead of apologizing. But of course she would know that because I never make salad unless that is all I am making, but I was still trying to get some response from her. "I always figure the spinach and spaghetti sauce are vegetables enough."

Still nothing. Ford just kept methodically cutting her square of lasagna into smaller, bite-sized squares and popping them into her mouth. I felt like she was eating in time to a metronome: cut, cut, stab, lift, pop, chew, chew, chew. And the whole time she also watched me.

"This is too fucking weird, Ford," I said, putting my own dinner aside. "For Christ's sake, talk to me."

"Okay," she said, popping the last of her lasagna into her mouth and bending to put her plate on the floor. "Okay. But you're not going to like it."

She pulled a leg up under her, a move I recognized as a signal for a from-the-hip discussion. Ford pulls no punches when she sits on her feet. I wondered for the hundredth time how a woman of her bulk could be so limber.

"I love you, Melanie."

"Melanie? Guess this is serious. You never call me —"

"Dead serious, honey. Long dead serious. Mel, you gotta stop this shit."

"What shit, Ford? Oh. You mean Camille. Investigating —"

"Investigating? Is that what you call it?

131

Obsessing is more like it. This has to stop. You have got to get a grip, girl. I don't want to be the one to tell you this, but as far as I can see, I'm the last living person you haven't cut out of your life, so I guess I have to. Honey, can't you see how this looks from my viewpoint? Here's this great woman, with a ton of potential and miles of opportunities everything, in fact, going for her — for you — and suddenly you're ... just blowing it all off. You withdraw from everyone, move out here to where the world drops off and then you get ... obsessed with a dead woman — a ghost — and now you've got me believing, but you've also got me scared and I can't believe — I just cannot believe — you aren't scared, too. You should be scared, dammit. Even Val said —"

"Val said what?" I began to protest, getting defensive. "She seemed pretty damned interested in what's going on here."

"Oh, yeah, she's interested. She's fascinated, Mel, but she's concerned too. Most people wouldn't stay in a ... situation like this unless they had to. You don't have to. Mel, honey, look. You are my best friend, my best bud. You are my family. You mean the world to me. I just can't sit by and watch what's happening to you."

"What? What's happening to me? Nothing. I am fine. I'm just fine."

"No, Mel. No, you are not just fine. You don't eat. You don't socialize. You don't —"

"I'm busy, Ford. Writing and school and —"

"Bullshit. When's the last time you attended any of your classes? And don't bother lying to me. I called the school. I talked to that professor friend of yours. She's really concerned about you, Mel. You could lose your fellowship, if you haven't already. And when's the last time you wrote anything, anything at all?"

"Ford, you know it doesn't work like that. Lots of my work is research. My work is solitary by nature. I'm —"

"You are full of shit. Research? You call digging up old newspaper stories research? You call spending all your time fixing up this shack research? You call obsessing about a dead woman research? You have got to stop this. You have got to get your life back. Mel, please listen to me —"

"Ford, you just don't understand."

"No. No, I do not understand. She is not even real. She's —"

"Yes, she is real. Camille is very real. She is more real to me than —"

"Than what?"

"Than most people."

"Than me? Is she more real to you than me? Because if the answer to that is yes, honey, you are in deep water, very deep, very dangerous water."

Ford sprang up and paced the room a few times. Then she resettled next to me on the couch, turned toward me with one knee resting against my thigh. She took both of my hands and squeezed. Tears filled her eyes.

"Mel, please. Please listen. You don't really know what you're dealing with here, what force. Val said something after we left here. She said there is definitely something here —"

"She told me that. Besides, it's some*one.*"

"Okay, okay. Someone. But after we left, on the way back to town, she also said that you need to be

133

careful. We can't really know what or who ... No, wait, let me finish. There are other theories, you know. I mean, maybe you don't know. I didn't know. I mean ... I've never thought much about this stuff — ghosts, spirits, demons, aliens —"

"Aliens? Who's talking UFOs here? There's just this lost soul, this young woman who died and lost the love of her life and hasn't gotten over it, hasn't stopped longing for —"

"Yeah, okay, that's what you believe. I want to believe too, really. It's better than —"

"What? Better than what?"

"Look. Val said some people believe — it's kind of bizarre, but some people believe all those things, all those 'visitations' come from the same place."

"Oh, yeah, right. Like Hell?"

"Well, not exactly, but sort of. Sort of ... another dimension. Sort of like a parallel universe where evil lives, evil forces. And these ... entities ... are all doing the same work, bad deeds, trying to spread misery and strife and ... well ... evil. Violence and ... well, the point is, nothing from that place can be good. Nothing good can come from —"

"Ford. Can you hear yourself? You think I'm off the deep end? We should be taping this conversation. Six weeks ago you didn't even believe in ghosts."

"Yeah, well, six weeks ago I wasn't scared of losing you, either. I'm trying to open my mind so would you, please, open your ears?"

I'd never seen Ford like that and it shook me. I wanted to appease her, to reassure her somehow.

"What is it you want me to do?" I asked.

"Move out of here, for one."

"No way."

"Get back on track at school."

"What else?"

"Get a goddamn phone. Get a girlfriend. At least get a date once in a while. I'd even rather see you back with that sociopath Becca than cut off like this."

"Well, actually . . . I did have a date."

Ford's face brightened for the first time. She grinned and punched me softly on the shoulder. "No shit. You did? When? Who?"

"Last night. The bartender at the bar I called you from. Bonnie. She . . . I hung out there waiting for you to call back and we got talking and . . . she came back here with me."

"Here? You brought her here?" Ford's face locked up for a second, then eased again slightly. "So . . . so what happened?"

"Well, nothing actually. I mean, I didn't bring her here to fuck her anyway. I mean, we were just talking. We just talked for a while."

"A long while?"

"Well, no. Not very long."

"What happened? Oh, hell, don't tell me. Let me guess. Camille. Camille scared her off, didn't she?"

"Well, not exactly. Camille didn't actually do anything. Bonnie, well, she just said she didn't like the . . . feel . . . the feel of the house. She wasn't comfortable. She . . . she left. She just upped and left."

"Uh huh," was Ford's only reply.

"But she said she'd call," I lied.

"Uh huh. Except for one thing, Mel."

"What?"

"You don't have a fucking phone, remember?"

135

* * * * *

The next morning after Ford left, I spoke to my not-at-all-empty house.

"Camille," I said, "We need to talk."

I made Ford's bed without changing the sheets — only she would ever sleep there — as I talked out her suppositions. Her words ran through my mind like severe weather warnings on the bottom of a TV screen, but for another county, far away.

"So, Camille, dearest one, are you some kind of demon?"

The thought made me laugh again. Camille. Funny, caring, giving Camille. Evil? "Yeah, right," I thought, answering Ford in her absence.

Whatever Camille was — ghost, other-dimension inhabitant or figment of my own imagination — I knew for certain she didn't have an evil ion in her. Her presence was as comfortable as Ford's. Maybe more so. Camille never questioned Ford's motives, her origins or place in my life.

I shared this thought out loud with Camille, who, I sensed, accompanied me as I tidied up the house.

"Also," I said, starting the water for the previous night's dishes, "you have never questioned her loyalties, have you? I'll talk to her about this. She just doesn't understand, does she? Well, give her time, she'll come around."

A fork I'd too quickly swabbed and put in to rinse lifted out of the water and returned to the wash side of the sink. Examining it closer, I saw a dried-on chunk of lasagna on its back.

"Sorry, Cam," I said, scrubbing more vigorously.

Then it sunk in and a shiver raised the hair on my arms.

"Oh shit. Camille? Camille, did you do that? Can you do that? Camille, can you do more things? Camille, do it again. Move something else."

Nothing more happened as my emotions careened from my initial incredulity to awe to delight and back again.

"Please, Camille, do it again. Move something."

Nothing.

Had I imagined it? Was I hallucinating? Did a fork float out of the rinse side into the wash? Was I crazy? Ford hadn't quite said crazy, not that exact word, but I did now. Was I?

Leaving the lasagna pan in the sink to soak, I went into the dining room and sat at the table, my head in my hands. I was shaken, my emotions roller-coastering. Surely, I reasoned, if Camille had this ability, she would have exhibited it before, wouldn't she? Why wouldn't she? Holding back? Wanting to surprise me? Keeping secrets? A thin edge of fear slipped through my consciousness. What else might she be keeping from me? What if Ford was — if not completely, at least partially — right? I could not accept the word *evil*, not about Camille, but what if she were more powerful than I had imagined? What if she were capable of ... more. And what, as Ford had asked before, exactly what did Camille want of me?

The familiar heaviness crept into my body and I dozed lightly as Camille's answers came to me. There was no voice, really, no words and phrases. It was more like thoughts, images. If she had used words, had used Rosa to answer my questions, they would have been: *Don't be afraid. I didn't know I could do that, either. I just thought of helping you do the dishes, of standing beside you helping with the dishes. I just thought of handing you that fork back and it happened. I've never done anything like that before. I am so happy I can do that. I don't know what else I can do. I've never tried. Let me try.*

I was aroused by a scraping sound on the table before me. The candle holder slid hesitantly to the right, then back, teetered slightly then settled.

"Too heavy," I mumbled, still groggy from the brief trance. Trance seemed to be the right word. Val had been right, I realized. But I was not afraid. I could not be afraid of my friend. I wanted in a dazed kind of way, to help her. "Try something lighter."

The curtain at the dining room window lifted, tenting out. I laughed happily. The curtain lowered and raised again, lowered and raised. Then the candlestick moved again but still only a slide. She hadn't lifted it off the table.

"Okay," I said. "You need to build up slowly. Stick with light things for a while, cloth maybe."

The air in the room shifted the way it did when Camille laughed. A corner of the rug folded up, then flipped back, then another and another, each of the four corners in turn. The afghan in the living room slid off the back of the couch as if by gravity, then slid along the couch seat.

On my makeshift coffee table, the glass bowl of dried rose petals tipped over and the petals swirled in the air as if by a tiny domestic whirlwind. I laughed out loud and stood up as the petals swirled toward and then around me, landing in my hair, on my shoulders, on my breasts. Then the hem of my T-shirt slid up my body, my back and midriff, followed by a slight, teasing pressure across my ribcage.

Struggling halfheartedly to preserve the last of my dignity, I wrestled with Camille for control of my shirt, laughing and scolding at the same time.

"Not funny, Camille. Stick to the curtains." But I wasn't really angry. Not this time.

Chapter 17

I never meant to hurt her. If only I'd known; if I'd been thinking. If, if, if.

It was early evening a week or so after Ford's visit and I'd been working around the perimeter of the living room, smearing patching plaster into cracks and crevices. It wasn't difficult work but tedious, and I was absorbed in doing the best I could at this newly learned skill. Earlier in the day I'd hacked off my cut-offs to make them even shorter, cut the sleeves off my work T-shirt and slit the neckline. Even with the doors and windows open

I couldn't catch the slightest breeze. Even for unpredictable Michigan, a heat wave in November was incredible. If I hadn't been premenstrual I might have used the intense heat as an excuse for a day off, but I had all this energy, this restlessness to harness, to channel. A girlfriend would have helped, maybe. Maybe not. I was so cranky I probably would have driven her off. Every minor difficulty — spilled plaster, too thin mix — angered me. Every time I had to move the ladder pissed me off all out of proportion. And that was another thing. The ladder. I know you aren't supposed to stand on kitchen chairs to reach high places, but I felt safer on chairs than on ladders.

It was just a six-foot aluminum ladder and I was sitting, not standing, on the second step from the top, filling a gap between the wall and the center beam. I didn't like being there, and the heat wrung salty sweat into my eyes. Sweat trickled down my spine and between my cheeks. My crotch itched with sweat and my underarm deodorant had long since surrendered. The damned ladder stood solidly but I felt nervous. I felt foolish, too. Here I was, putting my time and my money into a rented house that wasn't mine, would never be mine. The owners themselves didn't even care about it. I had my own work to do. Ford was right, I should be writing, reading, thinking at least. So I tried. As I filled and smoothed I tried to think about a story.

What if I wrote about this, just sitting on a ladder jamming plaster into the cracks of someone else's wall? Describe it. What kind of ladder? What kind of wall? What shade of white is patching plaster? What is its consistency? What does it smell like? Why would this character be doing this? What would it symbolize? Patching plaster as a metaphor for what? What does patching plaster mean to my character? Would it remind her of something? Someone? Would this uncomplicated act carry her somewhere else? In place? In time? And who, exactly, would my audience be? What would it mean to them? What could it possibly mean to them? What does anything mean to anyone? Does anything ever mean anything to anyone? Why? Did it matter what color her hair was?

I realized I was in a downward spiral and that the heat and my hormones were at least partially to blame. I put the pail of plaster and wide-bladed knife on the lip of the ladder and leaned back against the steps behind me. This is when accidents happen, I warned myself, when I'm outside myself, or way too deep inside, disconnected to the moment. After I relaxed a bit I'd take a bath, I thought, a nice slow, deliberate bath. With a few deep breathing exercises I tried to recenter myself. Eyes closed, head back, I inhaled slowly to the count of three, held it for three beats, exhaled to the count of three. I thought only about my lungs, my diaphragm like a party balloon.

Without warning, without scent or sound or shift of light or temperature, Camille's hand was on me, high on my bare, sweaty, plaster-freckled thigh. Too high, too sudden, too demanding. Hers was not a light flirtatious flicker, nor a sensuous stroke, but a firm, crude act of possession, of presumption, of right.

I snapped; snapped at her. "Go away! Leave me alone!"

Immediately I regretted it, knowing it would hurt her. It was a dismissal, a command, but one I hadn't planned. I had barked at her reflexively and cruelly. I never thought if I'd taken time to think that those five words spoken in that tone were all it would take to banish her.

I missed her so much. I didn't mean to drive her away. I never dreamed it would be so simple, a simple command spoken crossly. But she was gone. I didn't feel her, sense her, smell her perfume. I tried to conjure her, but nothing worked.

Night and day I kept Rosa on. I called her name. I even found a bottle of gardenia perfume and left its stopper off, hoping her own scent would summon her. But the perfume seemed harsh, artificial, only vaguely like her own.

Night after night I waited, longing for her return. A draft would lift my heart and hopes; a creak from the old house's ancient timbers would make me catch my breath in anticipation. I shouted to the ceiling and down the basement steps, "I'm sorry. I didn't mean it. I miss you. Come back. Come back, Camille."

Only silence and stillness met my efforts.

I finished taking down the suspended ceiling and hauled the parts to the barn in plastic garbage bags sealed with my purple duct tape. Maybe someday someone would want to replace it but I could not imagine why. The plank ceiling was dark and rich though the wood was rough, unsanded. The crossbeams were two-by-sixes, the hand-hewn timbers along the sides of the room fully exposed, thick and beautiful. I remembered what Camille had said about Sam carving her name on one and I finally found it, high up near the ceiling by the outside door. I fingered the shallow carved letters and wondered if Camille knew Sam had spelled her name with only one L.

I cried then — for Sam, for Camille, for myself. Misunderstandings break more hearts than cruelty, I thought, whispering her name again.

The dark ceiling diminished the light which had reflected off the white ceiling panels, but I liked it so much better. The planks of the ceiling were the planks of my bedroom floor, and occasional spaces let in slivers of light.

I'd started this job for Camille, but without her guidance I could not decide what to do next. The ceiling was unevenly dark and I thought about staining it with a sponge drenched in Old English but since that would take gallons, instead I began to peel off the vinyl wallpaper in the dining room. I thought Camille would approve, even if the landlady didn't, but there was no encouragement from her. Rosa remained silent, like a punishment.

The wallpaper peeled off so easily it made me wonder what had kept it on at all. Underneath was bare plaster, which surprised me. The stairwell's multiple layers had created an expectation of the same. I washed the walls down with bleach water and bought another carton of patching plaster for the few crumbled places. At every step I expected a hand on my shoulder or arm, a waft of floral approval. I was doing this for her. I was making Sam's cabin beautiful again, for her. Couldn't she at least show me a little gratitude? My sorrow was replaced by irritation. Where the hell was she? This was her goddamn house. So where was she? Once the plaster was patched, then what? What was I supposed to do then? What did she want? What did she want from me? What more could I do? Hell, I'd done everything, anything she'd wanted. So I got cranky once in a while. So what? She'd startled me and I reacted reflexively. I hadn't meant to hurt her feelings, to banish her. I get anxious on ladders, insecure. And she'd touched me so high up on my leg. It was too intimate, too surprising. And I was premenstrual, too. Didn't she ever get PMS?

Then I laughed. Yeah, right. A dead woman with PMS. And I was pleading with her, scolding her, begging her to understand. I was alone too much, I reasoned. Maybe I should spend the money, get a phone. Maybe I should have a party. Maybe Ford could come spend a weekend. But I knew she couldn't. A whole weekend off would have to wait until it snowed — heavily. Maybe I could go there? Change of scene, maybe meet someone. Maybe have a fling. I'd make some new friends. Or call some old ones from the corner, have them meet me somewhere. Maybe it wasn't too late for Bonnie. The idea sounded better and better. It sounded excellent. Yes. Old friends, new friends, music, lights, laughter. Bonnie. Yes. Company was just what I needed. I would make the effort. Maybe next week, the week after for sure.

First I needed to nail down the loose basement steps and give them a coat of paint.

* * * * *

Without Camille, the emptiness and sterility of the house seeped into my dreams. I dreamed I was walking in Owosso at 3 a.m. It was cold, damp, dark. I've never wandered around in Owosso, only stopped once at the Wendy's to get coffee on the way down to Ford's from Saginaw, but in my dream it was Owosso. I found a crystal shop still open. A woman saw me outside the shop, looking in the windows, and waved me in, but I refused and kept walking, cold and alone.

Most nights I could not remember my dreams but carried the flavor of them, or lack of it, into my days. Bleakness was the pervading sense of these dreams. I woke aching with loss, bordering on despair. I was more than alone, I was lonely. My preferred state became hateful to me.

Writing was impossible. No two words together looked right. Everything I attempted seemed flat, lifeless. I wanted only the one thing I could not have: Camille.

I could eat only a bite or two at a time and felt my clothes loosening on my body. I was obsessed, I realized, or worse. I was in love, hopelessly in love with a woman who'd been dead for eighty years and who inhabited my life more fully than I'd ever allowed a living woman to. I was in love with Camille. And I would wait forever if I had to for her to come home to me.

Chapter 18

It was still light, but only barely, when I got home. I'd gone out for yogurt and thermal transfer paper for Rosa, in case Camille came back. I'd filled the tank and even browsed the videos at the grocery store. All the movie titles were unfamiliar to me — where did all these movies come from? Looking back, I wonder if I sensed something and was stalling, or if I was, as I thought at the time, just dawdling.

I didn't recognize the car as I pulled up the driveway. It was light blue and boxy, expensive and not hers. Becca sat on the porch steps and neither of us spoke or moved until I approached.

She took off her ever-present sunglasses and asked, "Is it all right for me to be here?"

"Bek. How did you . . ."

"Got your change of address from the post office. Glad to see me?"

"You look like hell," I said.

"Should. Cry myself to sleep every night. Have since you left."

"You left."

"You kicked me out."

"I didn't take you back. You left."

"Same difference."

"No, Bek, no, it's not." I started toward the porch.

"You still mad?"

"It's not about mad. We just don't have anything left to talk about."

"Melly, please. Let me come in. I drove hours to get here."

"Go away. And don't call me Melly."

She grasped my arm. "Please."

There was a catch in her voice and when I looked down at her face, it was streaked with tears. She was always so ashamed of vulnerability. She could be happy or angry but she did not allow her sadness or hurt or need to show. I let her in because she cried and because she had a really bad haircut.

"What happened to your hair?" I asked. Not only was it hacked off in clumps but it was an uneven, intense black.

"Thought I needed something different," she said,

opening the refrigerator. "Got any beer? Could go get some."

"No, Bek. I don't have any and I don't want any and we've had this talk too."

"Yeah, yeah. Okay. Haven't changed any, have ya? This place is a dump."

"Yes, but it's my dump."

"You're still mad."

"No, I'm not still mad. I'm getting mad all over again. What exactly did you come here for, Bek? Why are you here?"

"Miss you. Thought you might be lonely. Heard you were still alone," she said with forced good humor, but what I thought she meant was, you still owe me.

"I don't owe you anything, Bek. Not one damn thing."

"No?" she asked with the old familiar snarl. Then she shrugged. "Maybe not. Maybe I owe you. We're still connected, Mel. I miss you. Can't we work it out?"

"There is nothing to work out. We were all wrong from the beginning. It was a mistake, a stupid mistake."

"You hate me," she whined, starting to cry again and slipping down into a chair.

I wanted to say yes. Yes, I hate you. I hate me around you. I hate how we are together, what we bring out in each other. I hate the way I let you treat me . . . in bed and out. I hate your meanness, I hate your stupidity, I hate your damn beer. I hate your parents and how you live and your values. I hate your lacks and your excesses and your . . . teeth. I hate that you have never had a cavity in your life

149

and you never get sick, not even a cold, but you do not take care of yourself at all.

"You do, don't you?" she said, interrupting my inner tirade.

"Hate you?" I lied, "No. I don't hate you. But I do hate your hair."

"Fix it?" she asked, grabbing a handful. She gave me that sheepish, goofy look that always made me laugh and forgive. A woman in tears and a chance to cut hair. I could not refuse.

"Okay," I said. "Okay, okay, okay."

"Let me take you out to dinner first?" she offered. "To thank you."

"Be seen in public with you in that hair? No way."

"Then I'll go get us something. There's nothing in the fridge but that shit you eat. Where's a store?"

I told her, and as she left she kissed me quickly on the cheek.

"See," she whispered, "just like old times."

While she was gone I sat in her chair thinking about those old painful times, and wondering why the hell I was letting myself get sucked in again even though I promised myself that nothing was going to happen.

Just like old times, she brought back two steaks large enough to feed two families and a twelve pack of beer brewed by a corporation whose chairman of the board was fascist. Two cans were already gone and she popped the tab on a third.

As I lemon peppered the steaks she opened another beer and handed it to me. For a second I hesitated but then took the can and swigged hard out of it. She watched me, smiling.

"That's a good girl," she said. "Tastes good, doesn't it? I want you mellow, baby."

I knew what she meant, what those words meant, but I refused to acknowledge them. The beer did taste good. The first third of an icy cold beer after a long drought always tastes good. But after the initial quench, drinking is an unpleasant chore for me. I'd learned to enjoy the part I enjoyed and to fake the rest — carry the same can around for hours or put it down somewhere still two-thirds full or dump it down the drain and refill the can with cold water. No one has ever caught on to those tricks, certainly not Rebecca. Her single-mindedness toward beer obscured what few powers of observation she possessed. This night was no exception.

She downed another can while making the salad. Her version of making salad was quartering a head of lettuce and pouring dressing on each wedge. After the salad was done I had her set the table while I finished broiling the steaks.

Bek talked about her new job selling used status and collectible cars. She was encouraged to drive them home, get them seen on the road, but there was a mileage restriction. She disconnected the odometer for days like this when she made longer trips than allowed. As she explained the technique she returned to the kitchen, rubbing her arms.

"Hell's bells, Mel, it's colder than a witch's tit in there. You got an air conditioner on or something?"

I followed her back into the dining room as if needing to confirm or investigate her complaint. But I knew the source of the cold. I knew, or hoped I knew, who was there. I contemplated denying there was anything wrong or different in the room, but it

151

would have been ludicrous. The air was icy. We could see our breath. Bek was stepping in and then back out of the room to test the boundary of the cold.

"It's okay," I told her. "The house is just haunted."

"Jesus Christ, Mel," she kept repeating, popping another beer and downing it in one long gulp.

I remembered the steaks and went back to pull them, trying to act as if nothing unusual was happening. But I was worried. That Camille was back thrilled me, but the cold . . . the cold was not good. Rosa sat, silent, on the corner of my desk.

How much to tell Bek was the question. How much did she want to know? How much would not be a betrayal of Camille's trust? My decision was shaped by Bek herself.

"Well, hell," she said, "you don't really believe in that shit, do you? You're supposed to be so goddamn smart, too." She laughed and reached for another beer.

"I'm not hungry anymore, not for food anyway," she said, leering at me. By her sixth beer she always wanted sex. She put the can down on the counter and moved closer.

It began when I let her in the house. I knew it was building to this. I knew her, her pattern, and mine with her. I knew food was a bed present. I knew about the beer. I knew things could get ugly if she didn't get her way. She was dangerous, not just her physicality, but because she elicited something inside me — compliance, yielding, mindless sexual response — that frightened me. I knew her faults and her twisted perceptions, but my body heedlessly responded to hers. I knew well the contradictions of her body — narrow shoulders, heavy breasts, slender back, large ass, heavy thighs, flat stomach, small waist. I knew exactly how she would kiss me, clasp me, squeeze and bite. I knew exactly how she would use me — rough and long, leaving bruises and aches. I knew the vile names she would call me when she came and I knew how abruptly she would leave when she was done. I'd be alone and used up in my bed, ashamed and humiliated. And I would let her, because part of me that lives in a dark, cold, scary place would revel in her roughness.

"Remember how much I love you?" The words slurred. Her hands were steady, though, as she pulled me closer.

Looking back, I wish I could say I resisted her, that the separation had given me newfound strength. I wish I could have told her to fuck off. Instead, I told her to fuck me. I said the words she'd taught me to say, that gave her permission.

She pushed me hard against the counter edge, laughing that throaty laugh as she grabbed at me, groping roughly. I grasped the counter edge with both hands, and my eyes were closed in shame and desire when the first blow came, but I saw the rest.

Full cans of beer flew through the air, aimed at Rebecca. The first one hit her square in the back. It was an open one that she'd set down on the counter and it drenched her in beer. Another one, pulled from the open pack she'd left on the floor, hit her in the ass. One more sailed past us and smashed into the wall. She whirled around and the next one hit her above her right eye. Blood trickled down her face as she turned back to me.

Terror danced in her eyes. "What?" she screamed at me. "What?"

The steaks came flying, then the broiler tray.

"What the fuck!" she yelled, holding her hand to the cut on her forehead.

"Get out," I said, struggling to control a rising hysterical, joyous horror. "Get out now. Don't come back."

"What is it?" She was crying again, backing toward the door as spice bottles, silverware, glasses, plates and even the lettuce wedges barraged after her.

"Don't ever come back," I warned.

"What is it?" Bek sobbed as she trotted to the car and roared away.

Not until she was gone did the fury subside.

"It is Camille. My love. My Camille. Mine." And I smelled her sweet welcome perfume and felt seductive warmth envelop me.

Chapter 19

And so I came to understand the depth of her desire, her need. I knew what she wanted of me but I could not foresee what would come of my compliance. Would knowing have made a difference? I don't know. Maybe. Probably not. It's pointless to conjecture now. I did what I did and I can't or won't regret it. Like her, the memory of that night will live with me forever.

What I did, of course, was give myself to her. At dusk the next night I gathered every candle that I owned, arranging them and the oil lamp around the futon in the green room. Then I bathed slowly, as if for a real lover, a bodied one. To me, she was real, and I'd felt her anguish and her ire. She'd shared her story with me; we'd wept together and laughed. Only this act was left to consummate our love, for I knew finally that I did love her. I loved her in my life. I wanted her to stay with me, or go with me, but to be with me in any case, forever. I needed her at least as much as she needed me.

I oiled my body lightly with mineral oil, inexpensive and unscented, then I went through the house unplugging all the electrical appliances. I wanted the house to be as much like it would have been for them, that other day. I would be Sam for her.

Spreading the purple and red bear's claw quilt on the futon, I then slowly lit the candles and the oil lamp. Flickering flames played shadows on the walls and ceiling as I lay down to wait for Camille.

At first I thought to summon her, to invite or to beg, but something guided me otherwise. I neither spoke nor whispered her name. I closed my eyes and allowed the heavy trance-like state to overtake me. I imagined her walking across the yard toward the house, wearing a white dress and wide-brimmed straw hat.

She takes off the hat as she walks and with one hand unbinds her hair which falls across her shoulders and down her back. The wind blows her skirts and the pink ribbons of her hat, and she reaches to brush her hair out of her face.

She smiles as she strides gladly toward the cabin. Sam saw her this way, I realized, but Sam had not been able to give her what I could.

I could picture Sam there on the bed. She lies on her back across the bed with one foot still on the floor. Her jacket is draped over the back of the chair. One hand slides under a strap of her braces. The other arm is across her eyes and in her hand is the gun.

The door unlatches and opens and Camille's soft voice calls, "Sam? Darling, are you here?"

But Sam does not move. Camille is framed in the doorway and the fading light enters the dark room only enough for her to see her beloved.

At first she laughs. "There you are. You frightened me." She moves to Sam's side. Then she sees the gun, so close to Sam's head, and she gasps. "No Sam! No! Don't think of it!"

She tries to pry the gun from Sam's hand but Sam will not let go. Sam moves her hand, however, and rests the gun down by her side. The misery in Sam's face is profound and brings tears to Camille's eyes.

"Darling, it won't always be like this. Soon we will be together."

But still Sam does not speak, turning her gaze toward the wall.

Camille cups Sam's face, tracing its contours, then slowly touches Sam's chest. She is murmuring endearments to her, barely audible, soothing, reassuring. She unbuttons first Sam's braces, then, starting at the top, Sam's shirt. When she begins to unbind Sam's breasts, Sam grabs her hands, stopping her. Camille winces at the grasp, and at the fury enflaming Sam's face.

"Damn you," Sam says, "Damn you, damn you, damn you. Can you not see? This thing we want is not possible." She pulls Camille's quilt from the bed, throws it across the room, shouts, "Don't give me things. Don't do for me. Don't love me anymore. Loving me can bring you only pain. Pain is all I know and all I have to give. What then? Will we live forever in shadows? Will you share with me this lie that is my life? Do you not see that I belong in no world? Do you not see that I am nothing?"

Sam rises from the bed and paces the room. Each time Camille moves toward her Sam moves away, out of reach. Sam sits finally on the edge of the bed with her head in her hands. She is crying. Camille cries too as she kneels between Sam's feet, trying to calm her.

"But you are something. You are my love. You are my heart's desire. You are my life, Sam. Please, can't you see that? All we need is to be together. Once joined, we will find our way. We will know what to do next. Sam, please, please trust me. Trust this love I have for you. Let me be the world to which you belong."

With these words she slides Sam's shirt off and finishes unbinding her breasts. At first she hesitates to touch Sam. She looks for signs of displeasure in her face. Finding none, she tentatively touches Sam's breasts.

"Poor darling," she murmurs, "look how these bindings have marked your body." She massages gently but the air is charged. Sam is playing with a lock of Camille's hair, enchanted once more with its abundance. She gathers handfuls of hair and pulls Camille's face to hers. As their kiss deepens they move to lie together on the bed, Sam on her back,

Camille on her side, close to Sam. Sam's hands explore the contours of Camille's body, fumble for the tiny buttons. Camille slowly trails her hand down Sam's chest, down past the waistband of her trousers, slowly down.

Suddenly Sam shouts. "No! No! No, no, no." She pushes Camille away. The gun is in her hand again, pointed at her head.

Then it is Camille who screams, "No! Sam, don't! Please, please don't." She wrestles for the gun.

But Sam is raving, is out of control and barely coherent. "Worthless," she says, and "Freak" and "Don't deserve to live," and finally, over and over, "Rather be dead. I'd rather be dead."

Camille and Sam both sob, clinging to each other on the bed. Camille has the gun, but seems unaware of it. They cry together for a long time, then lie spent in each other's arms. Sam lies on top with her head on Camille's breast, her hands tangled in Camille's long hair.

It is Camille who speaks finally. "Sam," she whispers, "Sam, my love, my life. Take me with you then. I have nothing to live for without you. It is a way to be together forever."

She slides the gun into Sam's hand and guides the way to her heart. The gun and their hands are between them.

"I love you," Camille says, brushing the hair off Sam's forehead and kissing her there. She covers her face with kisses as their tears mingle. "Me first," says Camille. "Do me first then follow quickly. Hurry, love, I wait for you."

Sam begins to pull away. "Dearest, I can't —"

The gun goes off. Horrified, she rises from the bed. The gun is in Camille's hand. A bright red flower unfurls against the white lace dress.

Sam's scream echoes through the cabin and through the years to jerk me back into myself.

The flames flickered and what could have been a draft brushed my leg as her perfume filled the room. I saw nothing but felt her presence as I remembered my intent and relaxed back into the bed. I reached above my head stretching out fully.

First I felt a heaviness on the bed beside me, accompanied by a warmth — her presence. Invisible fingers began to stroke my arms, slowly, so slowly, then my face. Slight pressures —on my forehead, chin, lips — I sensed were her kisses. I lay still though unexpected tears escaped my closed eyes and pooled in my ears.

It was an accident, I whispered to her. *It was an accident.* Did she hear me?

The caresses continued. She stroked me everywhere, hesitantly at first, as if in exploration. My ankle, the inside of my elbow, behind my knee — I felt her touch. The strokes on my thighs, belly and breasts made me tingle. The hair on my arms, legs, neck stood on end not from fright, but from sheer pleasure, sheer excitement, sheer expectation. She brushed my nipples, repeating the gesture. I felt a fastening there, a suctioning. Her mouth. Oh, God, her mouth. My sides were stroked, slowly, my hips.

I opened my eyes and saw nothing. My own body was glistening with oil and goosepimpled with desire.

Phantom fingers trailed down my belly, increasing in their pressure. Instinctively I parted my legs, allowing anything, inviting anything. At the first touch I heard, or thought I heard, a gasp, but was it hers or mine?

Deeper and more insistent were the strokes. Sometimes she refrained from entering, instead pressing external pleasures. Shamelessly, I shuddered in response and something that felt like joy sparkled the room.

The heaviness then shifted, covering me, pressing me to the mattress. Instinctively, I reached to embrace her. My hands fell to my own body but the weight of her remained, shifting against my length like an invisible tide. I raised one knee to ease it. She stopped — confused perhaps? But then she began again, rocking on top of me and against my thigh as the stroking continued, harder, more demanding.

An intensity of energy flashed through the room. The flames flared and danced and in the newfound brightness I saw on the wall the shadow of my body lying prone, and with my shadow rocked another, slender, intent, with a wild unbound cascade of shadow hair. She raised up then and I saw the silhouette of her body, of her breasts. I watched the shadow of my hand reach up to cup her breast and where the shadows met, my hand met nothing. I heard a laugh, not mine, as she turned also to the wall, watching me grasp thin air instead of her. She reached out a hand and I did too. There was nothing tangible, but our shadow hands overlapped against the wall, a cool warmth against my palm. The weight on me shuddered as I had earlier, then fell against me. I felt the tickle of her hair against my nose and a pressure on my lips. There was a breathlike movement at my ear, but it was in my heart I heard the word.

"Forever," she said. "Forever."

Chapter 20

That early December night Camille made love to me was the night the weather changed. As abruptly as she was gone, our prolonged summer was too. Winter jumped in with a determination to make up for lost time, freezing the leaves on the trees before they could fall.

While I waited for Camille's return, I wrote her story. Maybe I hoped it would lure her back, entice her. Maybe I wanted to capture that episode before memory fogged and reason denied its reality. She did seem further from me with each passing day. I could not waste this experience, I knew. Maybe I had no choice.

As if possessed, I wrote, every day, all day, forgetting whether I'd eaten, falling onto the couch, asleep before I got there. I must have showered, changed my clothes, checked the mail. But I have only a vague memory of that. All I remember is sitting at Rosa for endless hours, impatient to write the next word, the next sentence, exasperated when her limited ten-page memory would fill and I'd have to print the text before I could go on.

I had to invent a fate for Sam. I toyed with having her stay in Camille's house, trapped in her doubly false identity and in skirts. I thought she could live out her life lonely and lying, hating to stay but afraid to leave. Or I could have had her marry, bear children whose children's children would one day own the cabin Camille had died in.

Or I could have had her commit suicide, maybe while lying in Camille's bed — a fitting criss-cross. It gave me a tremendous sense of power to construct revenges for Sam.

Yes, I knew it was an accident; I understood that. But it was an avoidable accident, I believed. It was a pointless tragedy invited by cowardice and duplicity. I could not forgive Sam any more than I could forget Camille.

In the end I wrote that she simply disappeared, which was no fiction at all. I went back to the newspaper office and read through more old issues of *The Courier*. In a news story dated three weeks following Camille's death, I found it:

"Miss Samantha Carr cousin of the late Camille Carr, left yesterday to return to her Chicago residence. She was visiting her cousin at the time of her untimely death, presumably by her own hand. Speculation regarding Miss Camille Carr's presumed suicide centers around a possible unrequited love affair with her hired man, Mr. Samuel Morehouse, who, according to Miss Samantha Carr, has not been seen since shortly before the tragic occurrence. Miss Camille Carr's lifeless body was discovered by her cousin in Mr. Morehouse's vacated premises on the edge of the Carr property. Readers will recall that Miss Camille Carr was herself left parentless by a tragic train accident a mere three years ago. Mr. Morehouse has not been located; Miss Samantha Carr has returned to Chicago; and Miss Camille Carr has joined her loving parents in their heavenly abode. Disposition of the property is pending."

So Sam just walked away, trapped in femininity. Did she cross back? I can't imagine the answer to that question. Maybe she kept a female identity as a kind of penance. That solution keeps coming to me, maybe because I prefer it. If I knew that Sam suffered for Camille's death, I could find some forgiveness for her. But what about those three weeks in Camille's house, posing as Camille's cousin? That seemed so cold, so calculating. Neither my visions of her nor Camille's descriptions made her seem that callous.

Maybe my manufactured scenario was, after all, accurate. In my manuscript I have Sam in a prolonged state of shock, operating on pure instinct, grief-stricken, nearly deranged from guilt. As in real life, I have her contact the police and report Camille's "suicide." Thoughtfully, they shield her from the horror of Camille's lifeless body. And cousin? Why not? They were like kin, like family. The dress? Why not? She was a woman, after all; had worn feminine clothing almost all her life.

The mourning time in Camille's house she spent sitting in Camille's room, lying on Camille's bed, kneeling before Camille's chiffonnier with her hands full of Camille's frothy clothes. She spent weeks crying, crying, crying. And she left carrying with her only the painting of the waxy white flowers that held the name of the only woman she would ever love.

That's the way I solved it, being kind after all. It seemed so real as I wrote it, as if I'd been there, watching.

When the manuscript was done — after twenty-three solid days and nights — I hand-carried it to Dr. Burnside with an apology. She started to speak as I stepped into her office, to scold me, maybe, or to question. But she stopped herself after one look at me.

"My God, you look like hell," she said.

Wordlessly, I handed her the manila envelope containing my manuscript. "I'm sorry," I told her. "I have no excuse except..." I motioned to the package in her hands. "I want to come back. To school. I want another chance. Please."

"Melanie, I can't promise...

"I know. I don't ask for promises, but I'll give one. If I can come back, keep...renew...my fellowship, I'll work so hard. I'll do anything, everything I have to. Please. Just say you'll consider it. And read this. I know it needs work but that's what I'm here for. Say you will. Say you'll consider it."

She nodded. "Okay. That much I will promise: I will consider your return. And I will read this. Very carefully. I'll need all the help I can get to convince the committee. Still . . . my word carries a certain amount of weight and there is one discretionary fellowship tucked away. Maybe . . ."

I turned to leave, fighting an almost overwhelming urge to hug her, when she stopped me.

"Mel, wait. Let me ask you one question. What if I can't get your fellowship reinstated? What will you do?"

I knew the answer to that, I'd already considered it.

"I'll do whatever I have to do. I'm not afraid of work. I'll get a job, pay my way, cut down to part-time — whatever it takes, Professor Burnside."

She smiled and shook her head, "You're supposed to call me Kate, remember?"

As I left her office, I felt free, hopeful, and determined.

Next I went to Ford's apartment. She took one look at me — I must have been smiling — and threw her arms around me. She picked me up and swung me around like someone else's baby. That night I stayed at her apartment, catching up, sampling her first attempt at pesto-from-scratch, and meeting her new girlfriend Kriss.

There hasn't been an answer from school yet, but it's only been a few days. And there is one more thing I absolutely must do.

I've just given myself a fresh haircut and am on my way down to the Artesian Wells to see Bonnie. I know she's there because I saw her robin's-egg blue Mazda as I drove by. Now, if only, if only she's still single.

A few of the publications of
THE NAIAD PRESS, INC.
P.O. Box 10543 • Tallahassee, Florida 32302
Phone (904) 539-5965
Toll-Free Order Number: 1-800-533-1973
Mail orders welcome. Please include 15% postage.

TRUE LOVE by Jennifer Fulton. 240 pp. Six lesbians searching for
love in all the "right" places. ISBN 1-56280-035-3 $9.95

GARDENIAS WHERE THERE ARE NONE by Molleen Zanger.
176 pp. Why is Melanie inextricably drawn to the old house?
ISBN 1-56280-056-6 9.95

MICHAELA by Sarah Aldridge. 256 pp. A "Sarah Aldridge"
romance. ISBN 1-56280-055-8 10.95

KEEPING SECRETS by Penny Mickelbury. 208 pp. A Gianna
Maglione Mystery. First in a series. ISBN 1-56280-052-3 9.95

THE ROMANTIC NAIAD edited by Katherine V. Forrest &
Barbara Grier. 336 pp. Love stories by Naiad Press women.
ISBN 1-56280-054-X 14.95

UNDER MY SKIN by Jaye Maiman. 336 pp. A Robin Miller
mystery. 3rd in a series. ISBN 1-56280-049-3. 10.95

STAY TOONED by Rhonda Dicksion. 144 pp. Cartoons — 1st
collection since *Lesbian Survival Manual.* ISBN 1-56280-045-0 9.95

CAR POOL by Karin Kallmaker. 272pp. Lesbians on wheels
and then some! ISBN 1-56280-048-5 9.95

NOT TELLING MOTHER: STORIES FROM A LIFE by Diane
Salvatore. 176 pp. Her 3rd novel. ISBN 1-56280-044-2 9.95

GOBLIN MARKET by Lauren Wright Douglas. 240pp. A Caitlin
Reece Mystery. 5th in a series. ISBN 1-56280-047-7 9.95

LONG GOODBYES by Nikki Baker. 256 pp. A Virginia Kelly
mystery. 3rd in a series. ISBN 1-56280-042-6 9.95

FRIENDS AND LOVERS by Jackie Calhoun. 224 pp. Mid-western
Lesbian lives and loves. ISBN 1-56280-041-8 9.95

THE CAT CAME BACK by Hilary Mullins. 208 pp. Highly praised
Lesbian novel. ISBN 1-56280-040-X 9.95

BEHIND CLOSED DOORS by Robbi Sommers. 192 pp. Hot, erotic
short stories. ISBN 1-56280-039-6 9.95

CLAIRE OF THE MOON by Nicole Conn. 192 pp. See the movie —
read the book! ISBN 1-56280-038-8 10.95

SILENT HEART by Claire McNab. 192 pp. Exotic Lesbian
romance. ISBN 1-56280-036-1   9.95

HAPPY ENDINGS by Kate Brandt. 272 pp. Intimate conversations
with Lesbian authors. ISBN 1-56280-050-7   10.95

THE SPY IN QUESTION by Amanda Kyle Williams. 256 pp. 4th
Madison McGuire. ISBN 1-56280-037-X   9.95

SAVING GRACE by Jennifer Fulton. 240 pp. Adventure and
romantic entanglement. ISBN 1-56280-051-5   9.95

THE YEAR SEVEN by Molleen Zanger. 208 pp. Women surviving
in a new world. ISBN 1-56280-034-5   9.95

CURIOUS WINE by Katherine V. Forrest. 176 pp. Tenth
Anniversary Edition. The most popular contemporary Lesbian
love story. ISBN 1-56280-053-1   9.95

CHAUTAUQUA by Catherine Ennis. 192 pp. Exciting, romantic
adventure. ISBN 1-56280-032-9   9.95

A PROPER BURIAL by Pat Welch. 192 pp. A Helen Black
mystery. 3rd in a series. ISBN 1-56280-033-7   9.95

SILVERLAKE HEAT: A Novel of Suspense by Carol Schmidt.
240 pp. Rhonda is as hot as Laney's dreams. ISBN 1-56280-031-0   9.95

LOVE, ZENA BETH by Diane Salvatore. 224 pp. The most talked
about lesbian novel of the nineties! ISBN 1-56280-030-2   9.95

A DOORYARD FULL OF FLOWERS by Isabel Miller. 160 pp.
Stories incl. 2 sequels to *Patience and Sarah*. ISBN 1-56280-029-9   9.95

MURDER BY TRADITION by Katherine V. Forrest. 288 pp. A
Kate Delafield Mystery. 4th in a series. ISBN 1-56280-002-7   9.95

THE EROTIC NAIAD edited by Katherine V. Forrest & Barbara Grier.
224 pp. Love stories by Naiad Press authors. ISBN 1-56280-026-4   12.95

DEAD CERTAIN by Claire McNab. 224 pp. A Carol Ashton
mystery. 5th in a series. ISBN 1-56280-027-2   9.95

CRAZY FOR LOVING by Jaye Maiman. 320 pp. A Robin Miller
mystery. 2nd in a series. ISBN 1-56280-025-6   9.95

STONEHURST by Barbara Johnson. 176 pp. Passionate regency
romance. ISBN 1-56280-024-8   9.95

INTRODUCING AMANDA VALENTINE by Rose Beecham.
256 pp. An Amanda Valentine Mystery. First in a series.
ISBN 1-56280-021-3   9.95

These are just a few of the many Naiad Press titles — we are the oldest and
largest lesbian/feminist publishing company in the world. Please request a
complete catalog. We offer personal service; we encourage and welcome direct
mail orders from individuals who have limited access to bookstores carrying
our publications.